Mrs. Alexander

A Choice of Evils

Vol. II

Mrs. Alexander

A Choice of Evils
Vol. II

ISBN/EAN: 9783337052829

Printed in Europe, USA, Canada, Australia, Japan

Cover: Foto ©Andreas Hilbeck / pixelio.de

More available books at **www.hansebooks.com**

A CHOICE OF EVILS.

A Novel.

BY

MRS. ALEXANDER,

AUTHOR OF

"THE WOOING O'T," "FOUND WANTING,"
"A WOMAN'S HEART," "FOR HIS SAKE," Etc.

IN THREE VOLUMES.

VOL. II.

LONDON:

F. V. WHITE & CO.,
14, BEDFORD STREET, STRAND, W.C.
1894.

PRINTED BY
KELLY AND CO. LIMITED, 182, 183 AND 184, HIGH HOLBORN, W.C.,
AND MIDDLE MILL, KINGSTON-ON-THAMES.

CONTENTS.

CHAP.   PAGE

I.—CRUMPLED ROSE LEAVES .   .   .   1

II.—"THE DAY IS COLD AND DARK AND
     DREARY "   34

III.—A WINTRY SUN   68

IV.—LIFE'S FITFUL FEVER .   .   .   89

V.—A CRISIS   123

VI.—ON THE RACK   149

VII.—A DECREE NISI   .   .   .   172

VIII.—AN INTERLUDE   190

IX.—BREAKING AWAY   211

A CHOICE OF EVILS.

A CHOICE OF EVILS.

CHAPTER I.

CRUMPLED ROSE LEAVES.

With daylight came common sense.

Janet sent a few pleasant affectionate lines to her husband and busied herself about many things, for the greater part of the day, delighting her father's heart by going to dine with him.

As she arrived two hours at least before the Captain's dinner time, he was enabled to ask the Vicar, his wife, and the daughter who was to replace Mary, the curate, and an old employé of the bank—a crony of the host's—to an impromptu little dinner, which was all the more delightful because of its un-expectedness,—for which Captain Rowley inspected the making of the curry, while Mrs. Palliser of Mervyn Hall, laid the cloth and arranged the beautiful fruit and flowers she had brought. It was quite a lively repast, and the hospitable old sailor was in his glory.

This was much better than moping at the Hall alone, thought Janet, as she looked round, and then a slight feeling of surprise passed through her mind as she felt how much she loved the little old cottage, which had been her home. No! delightful as her beautiful new abode was, it should never banish the old one from her heart.

Palliser was late in returning, another telegram told Janet he had missed the train, so dinner was turned into supper, and about nine o'clock, the sound of wheels made her heart beat wildly. With some difficulty she kept herself from running out to the hall, to throw herself into his arms. But her instinctive knowledge of his thoroughly English horror of scenes, of any display of affection before the servants, held her back.

The next moment, she heard his voice
speaking to someone, someone who was an
equal—she knew the tone, and a sudden sense
of disappointment fell upon her.

Then the door opened, and Palliser crossed
the threshold, saying as he did so:

"I have brought a guest whom you
will be pleased to see," as if to warn her
against demonstrativeness, while behind him,
the broader, square figure, and bold frank
face of Lord Darrell appeared.

And she was to welcome *him* instead of
relieving her heart by a burst of tears!

"This is an unexpected pleasure!" she
struggled to say it brightly. "I hardly
hoped you would come with Mr. Palliser,
though he promised to persuade you to pay
us a visit." She was quickly recovering
herself.

"Many thanks, Mrs. Palliser. It was a
sudden thought on Palliser's part, and I was
very pleased to come. Sorry we kept you
waiting! What a salubrious spot Mervyn
Hall must be! You look more blooming even

18*

than you did in town in spite of the hot weather."

" Or seems so, " put in Palliser; " you can't fancy how ghastly most of the women looked, after the racket of the season, especially coming in on the fag end of it, as I did."

" And still more especially, considering the roses and lilies you left behind ! " added Darrell with a good-humoured smile.

" It was amusing though," resumed Palliser. " I went to three dinners and the other days I was in the Strangers' Gallery. Heard Gladstone and Hartington, and several howling Irishmen."

" And longed to add to the clamour," said Janet, slipping her hand into his, as she thought unseen by Darrell.

" No," replied Palliser, pressing it hastily and instantly releasing it, " not for a long time, not till I have mastered the shibboleth ! Come, Darrell, let us get rid of as much dust as we can before we sit down to table."

Janet walked to the window, and gazing

out into the moonlight, took herself severely
to task for her own fancifulness, but why—
why did Randal bring a visitor back with
him! If he had even come to-morrow, if
they had had even one evening to stroll out
and talk all by themselves. But she must
not expect a man to be satisfied with the
monotony of tenderness and affection which
filled her own life to overflowing. Indeed
she felt that a man would not be worth
much who could be so content; she might in
time even weary of it herself, but, why—
why—did he bring Darrell with him?

By the time the gentlemen joined her, Janet
was herself again, and the trio talked gaily
over their repast, retailing all the latest gossip
for her benefit, and explaining Darrell's
yachting plans.

His new vessel had only just been launched
and the fittings and furniture were not yet
complete. "Then," continued Lord Darrell,
"I should like to take a short trial trip to
see how she behaves at sea, before I venture
to take so distinguished a passenger," bowing

to Janet, " on board, so it may be quite the first or second week of July before we can hoist the Blue Peter ? "

" A very good time," said Palliser, passing the claret, " we'll have a thunderstorm or two, but we have brave hearts, have we not, Janet ? "

" No doubt," cried Darrell. " Mrs. Palliser looks as if she were game right through ! Now, as to the party, I should like a few choice spirits. I haven't room for many. Who would *you* suggest ? "

" I have no suggestion to make," said Janet colouring. " I do not know anyone enough to judge whether they would stand the test of being shut up with unless, indeed, Lady Saville ? "

" My aunt ! " cried Darrell, " excellent. I did think of asking her, she is always charming—my uncle is inaccessible, so let him remain. Now, Palliser, name some man ! Though the selection ought to go the other way round."

" There's Danby and Fairfax, and—oh !

lots of fellows, you know best, you ought to choose your own guests!"

"So I shall, some of them! Danby might do! Come, Mrs. Palliser, have you no fancy man?"

"I think not," returned Janet with a smile.

"That is impossible—try, try, try again!"

"Well, then, I used to enjoy talking to Sir Peter Lyons whom we met at——"

"What! Lyons!" interrupted Darrell, "why, this is tremendous! Do you want to sink my poor little craft with such weight of metal as Sir Peter Lyons! the great anthropologist! Pray pass me the water, Palliser! I am overcome! Do you mean to say that you ventured to talk calmly face to face with that monster of learning and philosophy? I quite stand in awe of *you*, my dear Mrs. Palliser!"

"He is exceedingly nice and concealed his appalling acquirements successfully. Indeed, I found him quite kind and sympathetic!"

"I daresay you exercised some spell over

him, but for mere commonplace creatures such as Palliser and myself it would be too terrible a prospect. I should feel as if I had caught an elephant in a butterfly net. No, my dear Mrs. Palliser, anyone but Lyons!"

"Very well," said Janet laughing, "I give up Sir Peter, and feel ashamed of my blunder, but really, I liked him immensely."

"I only hope Mr. Palliser will not develop into a lion-hunter," said her husband. "This idea of hers is rather prophetic," and they went on to laugh and talk over the proposed yachting party, till Janet, finding it later than she thought, said good-night, and left them to their cigars.

"Oh, Randal," she exclaimed, when at last she had a word with him alone. "*Why* did you bring him down with you?— to-morrow would have done as well!"

"Eh — why? Oh, I don't know. He rather wanted to come, and can only stay two or three days! I thought you liked Darrell?"

"Yes, I do, but——"

" I saw old Digby when I was in Town," interrupted Palliser, quite heedless of her tender reproach, " and he is certainly looking better, but he told me he was pretty well sick of active life, only he wanted to keep the county open for some better Liberal than himself. I don't fancy he thinks I have an idea of standing."

And Janet listened eagerly as her husband enlarged on this all-important topic, while she blushed at her own folly in expecting Palliser to attach the same importance to his return and the joy of meeting as she did.

The day following, Darrell was carried off to the Home Farm to inspect the intended improvements, and interview the architect who was already measuring and sketching plans.

Janet therefore had her morning to herself and added some pages to her record of those delightful days of travel and of bliss, of which she was anxious to preserve her impressions, also to write a second long letter to her friend Mary, asking for information as to her plans, as she (Janet) feared her yachting expedition might prevent her being present at the wedding.

The gentlemen were a little late for luncheon, and Lord Darrell was profuse in his apologies.

"What a charming place this is," he continued. "It must be more than ten years since I saw it, and I had forgotten it. It is so thoroughly English, the trees are magnificent! The Pallisers must always have had lots of ready money, or the woods would have suffered more than they have done."

"I believe your own place is beautiful, Lord Darrell," said Janet.

"It is in a pretty country and has the advantage of a small river running through it, but it is altogether of the villa order—small and pretty; my grandfather, the first lord, bought it, we have not lived on the land like the Pallisers, a thousand, or is it two thousand, years?"

"Say five hundred, and perhaps you will be over the mark," returned his host, smiling.

"No matter. You are the real aristocrat. My people were of the cottonocracy, still, they managed to make things pretty comfortable for *me*."

"You ought to see the show place of Southshire, Darrell, that is, if you have never seen it—Clare Castle."

"No. I meet the owner occasionally, but he has never had the sense to invite me."

"We can ride over this afternoon, if you like. There is a good deal of shade all the way, and we need not start till four."

"Very good, I should like to see it. You'll come with us, Mrs. Palliser? Being country-bred of course you ride."

"I have ridden very little, but I enjoy it immensely. I only fear I might be rather in your way."

"Nonsense, my dear Mrs. Palliser! It would be the greatest addition to our pleasure."

"Perhaps, Randal," she said, "I might ride that nice, quiet, old horse I used to have when Lady Saville was here. He would want no management."

"No, I don't fancy you are practised enough to ride with Darrell, who is one of the crack riders in Leicestershire. I am afraid Mrs. Palliser began too late to do much in the equestrian line."

"I don't believe it! She is the very cut for a horsewoman! Don't mind him, Mrs. Palliser—come with us, and *I'll* look after you!"

"I wish you would let me try, Randal?" said Janet imploringly. "I did so enjoy the rides I had. I should have asked you before, only you did not seem inclined to ride yourself."

"What a hard-hearted fellow you must be, Palliser, to say 'No' to your wife! You come down in your habit at four, Mrs. Palliser, and depend upon it, you'll find your horse ready."

Janet glanced at her husband, and noticed a displeased look in his eyes, which she began to know.

"I hate to see women on horseback. They rarely ride well, and when they do, they look masculine, which is always hideous," he said contemptuously.

"My dear fellow! you are talking rank heresy! A woman never looks more charming, than when swaying easily to the motion of her horse. Look at your sister?"

"Yes, I know the fuss people used to make about her, but—I have no wish that *my* wife should resemble her!"

"Oh, I grant that it is better that Mrs. Palliser should be herself than resemble any one else, but Lady Saville is admirable on horseback."

"She is indeed!" exclaimed Janet. "It is a pleasure to look at her."

"Well," observed Palliser shortly, "I am quite sure it would not be a pleasure to look at *you* in the present stage of your experience, so for the present, do not attempt to ride. Hereafter——"

"Oh, very well," returned Janet good-humouredly. "If you leave me a loophole of hope, that you will undertake to perfect me in—what is the usual number?—six, or

let us say twelve lessons, given in the strict
privacy of our own park—I shall be content,
and will not insist on making an exhibition of
myself to-day."

She stole a glance at her husband, hoping
to read some loving acknowledgment in his
eyes, but the cold, annoyed look had not left
them.   A swift sense of fear crisped Janet's
nerves—was he going to be cross and easily
offended? Was she going to be uncertain
of herself—of her position with him? She
must not allow such a weakness to master
her !

"By Jove, Palliser, you are on the high
road to ruin," cried Darrell, "if your wife
gives up to you in that fashion."

"It is not a great renunciation," returned
Palliser icily, and rising from the table, he
added, " I shall order the horses then at four,
and if you will excuse me, I have some
matters to attend to."

" Of course ! it's all right."

" Will you come and sit under the trees,
Lord Darrell?" asked Janet.   " I think it is

cooler than indoors, all our sitting rooms are on the sunny side of the house."

" It will be delightful."

Darrell lit his cigar, while Janet put on her hat in the hall, and took a mesh of delicate knitting to occupy her hands while she talked.

" This is heavenly," said Darrell, settling himself in a deck chair from which he had a good " three-quarter " view of Mrs. Palliser's expressive face. "There is a wonderful air of repose about you, do you know ? It makes a fellow wonder why he ever bothers about anything, and that knitting, or whatever it is, takes off the dreary look of idleness. I'm not idle myself, still, I cannot cheat Satan ! He finds a heap of mischief for my busy hands to do."

"Then you must occupy them more diligently with what is *not* mischievous, Lord Darrell ! "

" Yes ; but with what?—there's the difficulty." He paused, and smoked a minute in silence. "Now," he continued, " I am going to read you a lecture. I am one of the family, you know, in a sort of way—shall I say—a sort of cotton back, to the superior satin face?—and Palliser, we must allow, has a most superior gloss! But, my dear kinswoman, you give him his head too much. He'll get out of hand altogether; you should have stuck to the riding whatever happened."

"What! vex Randal about such a trifle!" cried Janet.

"Nothing is a trifle that establishes a precedent," returned Darrell, sententiously. "The next time you want anything you'll find it ten times harder to get it. My dear Mrs. Palliser, men are great brutes, and born tyrants, every man of them! The more a woman gives in to us the less we value them; a melancholy fact, but the truth. Look at my uncle Saville, his wife worshipped the ground he walked upon, and see what came of it."

"That I do not know, but I fear they might be happier!"

"Well, yes, they might."

"But," continued Janet with fire, "you

could never compare Sir Frederic Saville with Palliser."

"No, Palliser is a superior article altogether! Yes, I really mean it. A high-bred gentleman—but don't give in to him too much!"

"You ought to be ashamed of preaching rebellion to the wife of your friend," said Janet, smiling. "What should you do or feel if you were married and your wife insisted on riding in opposition to you?"

"If I ever cared enough for any woman to marry her, I should want her to ride with me every day."

"Never mind that, put yourself in Randal s place."

"Well, do you know, I almost wish I could," he returned, with a frank, amused look that made Janet laugh. "Suppose then I had an objection to my wife's riding, and she persisted in it, why, I'd swear a big swear, I daresay, and the next time I wanted to be backed up in any way, I'd think my wife is a backer worth having. If she yielded like an

angel, as you did just now, I'd give her a
dozen kisses on the first opportunity (I'm
rather an affectionate fellow), and insist on
having my own way next time we differed,
more tyrannically than ever! That's human
nature, my dear Mrs. Palliser!"

Janet was greatly amused. She was blessed
with a sense of humour—a precious gift,
which is the salt of the mind—saving it from
insipidity, and drawing out the true flavour of
all mental comestibles.

Then Palliser was seen coming to join them,
and the conversation was at end.

Darrell stayed a day or two longer than he
intended, and seemed quite happy, in spite
of the absence of sport or any other amuse-
ment.

Janet liked him greatly, he was blunt, yet
never rude, and his candid views respecting
the true value of things were original and
diverting.

Palliser liked him also, yet his brow often
contracted when he noticed how rapidly his
young wife was growing intimate and at home

with a man who was somewhat formidable to the society amongst which he moved for his outspoken contempt of shams, still his evident pleasure in her society flattered the husband's vanity, which was a large ingredient in his character, and man's company is always gain to a man, when the first effervescence of a love fit is over. All particulars of the yachting expedition were fixed, Lady Saville willingly accepted Darrell's invitation, as her eldest son had decided to join his father in Norway.

The new buildings proved a godsend, in providing occupation and interest, which Janet shared heartily. Palliser rode out more frequently, but when Janet smilingly reminded him of his implied promise to teach her, she met a curt refusal, and, a little wounded, she did not return to the subject.

Time flew fast and the date fixed for their cruise drew near. Janet found she could not be home in time for her friend's wedding, and was obliged to content herself by choosing a handsome and useful present for her, when

they went to London to get some suitable
yachting garments, before joining *The Sea
Bird* at Cowes.

On the pains, the pleasures, the social
delights or difficulties of a yacht's cruise we
will not dwell ; are they not written in the
fascinating pages of W. Black ?—so that he or
she whose " soul might sicken o'er the heaving
wave," may enjoy it all in their easy-chairs.
Enough to say that it was, on the whole, a
highly successful expedition.

Perhaps none enjoyed the cruise more than
Janet did, on the whole ; it was a totally new
experience to her, and she was popular with
her fellow passengers. She thoroughly appreciated the sea and the fine coast scenery, but,
looking back over these days afloat, when she
sat down to the reprehensible occupation of
scribbling her " impressions "—she recollected
a good many unpleasant ones—when Palliser
was considerably ruffled—she was not always
quite sure why — certainly, when she
neglected to keep her veil down, and was
tanned by sun and air, for fair skins are apt

to become red under such treatment. He was annoyed by her carelessness,—no doubt it *was* careless on her part to neglect her appearance for one moment, and her husband's anxiety that she should look her best was flattering, but, at the same time, rather tiresome.

These little gusts and eddies of temper were sweeping up misty cloudlets from the horizon of the future, which shrouded the heavenly light of other days—days so near in time—so far away by the measurement of the heart. Still, she would not allow herself to be morbid or fanciful. Randal loved her dearly, and that was enough. For the rest, if he had the serious interest of a political career, he would have no time for faddles.

They had, without much difficulty, persuaded Lady Saville to return with them, and, at Janet's suggestion, Palliser invited her younger boy to spend the holidays at Mervyn Hall.

Palliser was certainly attached to his sister, yet sometimes spoke to her with a degree of harshness that surprised Janet; moreover, she often said to herself, "If Tom dared to address me in such a tone I should pull him up very sharply!" Another little crumpling of her rose leaves was occasioned by her wish to invite her brother and his wife for a brief visit to the Hall before the summer was quite over.

In truth she was not particularly anxious for their company; though always friendly with her brother, she was not deeply attached to him—the differences between them were too fundamental for intimacy, but she knew so much courtesy was due to him. Now she found it was a desperate effort of courage to open the subject to her husband. She knew he did not particularly like Tom, and would consider Mrs. Tom hopelessly bourgeoise. Still, it was a duty to ask his leave, at any rate,—and she would.

As she made this valiant resolution, it flashed across her mind that had she been in her old home—her real home, as she felt it to be—she would certainly out of respect and

politeness have asked her father's permission
to invite a guest, but she was perfectly assured
of the reply. Then came the question—if
Mervyn Hall was hers as well as Randal's, if
she were the mistress, as he was the master,
why did she feel this hesitation? The answer
came quickly — everything in it was her
husband's, the very clothes she wore were his
gift, she was penniless and, metaphorically,
naked, but for him; therefore she could *not*
be his equal. True, she might be his heart's
delight—he might love and cherish her,
indeed; he had always been chivalrous and
generous, but though she was his, and had a
legal right to share his life and all that he
had, she was but a pensioner on his bounty,
and the eternal materialism of things forbids
belief in the fable of equality when it does
not stand firmly on the solid basis of
£. S D. or equivalent advantages.

These were unworthy thoughts—perhaps
she was naturally low - minded, but for a
moment she realised what unspeakable degradation it must ever be to the individual

who is completely dependent on another, no
matter how dear or how good—except only a
parent. Still, dependence on a husband was
not considered dependence, and who was she
to set her uneasy fancies against the wisdom
of the past, the prevalent opinions of the
present? Only she must not be exacting,
she must not worry Randal—the tenderness
of her affection would prevent that—but also
because the paymaster had a right to turn
round and say at any moment "This or that
must not be."

"But a look at his dear face will banish all
these crooked fancies," thought Janet, as she
sound of Palliser's voice reached her from the
garden beneath; she would cast all her doubts
and fancies to the winds, and ask her kind,
generous husband for what she wished. If
he refused, she would be sorry, but she would
have done her duty.

She locked away her writing and descended
to meet him. He was giving some directions
to the gardener and looking well and bright.

"Come with us," he cried, as she descended

the steps from the drawing-room window.
"I think this corner might be cleared of
trees a little — it would give a peep at
the old church tower, and make a pretty
vista."

Janet accompanied him across the grounds,
entering with warm interest into his plans.
After some discussion, and giving definite
instructions to the head gardener, they
returned to the house, and halted in the
drawing room, expecting the gong to sound
for luncheon.

"Randal," said Janet, coming to where he
had thrown himself into a lounging chair, and
smoothing his hair gently, "I should like to
ask Tom and his wife here for a few days
before the shooting begins."

"Your brother—here!"

There was horror in his voice.

"Yes. I was afraid it would bore you, but
I want to be a little polite, and they need not
stay long."

"Good Heavens! they cannot stay less than
a week, and—it will be an infernal bore! I

would rather have Captain Rowley here—a good deal!"

"Why, Randal! you don't think my dear father a bore?" in a tone of dismay.

"Wonderfully little of a bore considering his age and the life he has led! Come, Janet, don't be so weak as to imagine your geese swans, because they are *your* geese—you are by no means without sense, pray use it."

Janet felt dazed for an instant, she honestly believed that Palliser was fond of her father, and liked his society. Tears came to her eyes, but she forced them back; she was rapidly learning the necessity of conciliation.

"Of course, you do not feel towards him quite as I do," she said with a quick sigh. "But if it is not *too* great a bore, I *should* like Tom and his wife to pay us a visit, and while Gertrude is here, she is so kind and helpful, and——"

"She is a deuced deal too sympathetic and all that sort of thing," interrupted Palliser sternly, "at any rate for her own good. I hope *you* will not go off on that tack, Janet, it leads women into all sorts of weakness."

"I fear I am naturally sympathetic, Randal, but I shall try to be stern and stony! Well, if it is intolerable to you, we will say no more about Tom's visit at present, only I think you are a little too much afraid of trifling discomforts, and remember, a week's endurance would set you free for a year at least from any repetition of it."

"A year! am I to have these people once a year?"

"Not if you object so much—there, we will say no more about it."

She turned away more distressed than vexed, and went to the window by which they had just entered.

Palliser was silent for a minute, then he said harshly:

"Don't be silly and ill-tempered, Janet! I don't like to be bored—no man does! I naturally express what I feel to *you*, but it is as well to ask your brother and his wife here while we are comparatively alone, only make it clearly understood that it is to be a week's visit."

" Very well. I will write this afternoon."

There was a slight tremor in her voice, for she had been thinking what a revelation Palliser's present view of her father had been to her.

" Good God ! " he exclaimed with much disgust. " You are not weeping, are you, over this rubbish ? "

" Certainly not ! " said Janet, suddenly restored to firmness and composure, and turning to face him with head erect. " My tears are not quite so ready ! "

Something in her tone startled Palliser, but before he could speak the gong sounded. He rose and opened the door for his wife, saying as she passed : " Is there a dash of the vixen in you, Janet ? "

" I don't know. It might be an amusing variety ! " she returned good - humouredly. " Too much sweetness is cloying."

" Ah ! I do not want to be amused in that style ! The sweetness is still very sweet ! "

said Palliser, with a smile, and they went to table in a more harmonious mood.

Janet was, however, almost ashamed of her own sense of relief when a couple of days after the post brought her a reply from Mrs. Tom Rowley. They were much pleased by the invitation, but reluctantly obliged to refuse. Tom had just had rather a long holiday for their wedding trip, and was now obliged to stay in Town while his partner took his family to the seaside.

With laughing eyes Janet handed the letter to Palliser who, on returning it to her, observed with mock gravity:

" 'Virtue has its reward.' "

But though this slight ruffling of matrimonial bliss passed over with apparently little or no bad result, the idea that the dear old father was already more or less a nuisance to her husband, pressed heavily on Janet's heart. Formerly his kindly pleasure in talking to the Captain, in drawing him out and listening to his stories, or better still, in arguing with him as if he had the highest opinion of his judgment, was a source of the purest joy to her. He—really was more sympathetic, more considerate and respectful than Tom, by a long way. Why should he change? Certainly, he was always polite and observant to her father, but *did* he find him that most abhorred thing, "a bore"? If such a mental revolution had taken place, what state of mind, of affection, would be lasting?

Janet feared she should never enjoy the old man's visits thoroughly again—not with this consciousness that her husband was wishing him away tormenting her. Then came the recollection that Palliser had suggested Captain Rowley finding a more suitable abode at Beachurst; did *that* mean a wish to get rid of him? Impossible! she would not think about it. Dwelling on small worries only warped the mind and magnified mole hills.

Then Palliser soon after called on his father-in-law, and himself invited him to dine and stay the night, so the sun shone again in a blue sky for Janet.

Meanwhile, Lady Saville's sons (both had now joined them) were visitors after Janet's own heart. The eldest was a mixture of father and mother. Like the former physically, with a good deal of the latter's refinement and charm of manner. He was easy going and sure of himself, and was soon on terms of the happiest intimacy with his Aunt Palliser. It seemed so droll to her having a nephew barely two years her junior. The second boy was more than four years younger, and extremely fond of fishing. This had been Captain Rowley's chief sport, as it often is with men who cannot afford horses, or tips to gamekeepers, and the boy was delighted to have his guidance and hints, though the sturdy old sailor found his own "staying" powers were considerably diminished.

On the whole the summer and autumn passed quickly and smoothly. Palliser diligently cultivated popularity to such an extent, that he was absolutely civil and hospitable to his relative the banker and his family.

Lawn tennis parties, pic-nics, dinners, succeeded each other, and still Lady Saville lingered on in her comfortable quarters—to Janet's sincere satisfaction, as she gradually grew to feel that her sister-in-law was really the one person she could depend on.

Of Palliser she was never sure—sometimes he spoke and acted as if he were bitterly annoyed with her, and she quickly learned that nothing offended him more than to ask him the reason, especially as he had none to give.

Then again, he had fits of passionate fondness quite as unaccountable; these alternations slowly impressed Janet with the unpleasant conviction that she had no sort of sacredness in his eyes, as some women are taught that the kisses of to-day are no guarantee against the curses of to-morrow. Palliser, however, was a well-bred man and had enough surface self-control never to be guilty of the curses. He managed, however, to show his feelings very successfully without coarser indications.

Before the winter had begun, Janet had learned to guard both eyes and lips, her facial muscles, the intonations of her voice, while she struggled desperately to hold on to the affection she firmly believed existed, and to blind her own judgment by telling herself that her tact and perception were at fault, that she would improve in time, and that these clouds of misunderstanding would fade away before the sunshine of that love, which already lay a-dying.

CHAPTER II.

NOVEMBER was upon them, not dark and drear as that month so often is, but clear and crisp, if rather colder than it usually is at the beginning of winter. Hunting was already in full swing, and Lady Saville had at last induced Sir Frederic to decide on a winter residence. Their own place was let on lease to a wealthy China merchant, and their town house was on the books of more than one West End house agent.

They were in fact expiating a career of more than usual folly and extravagance, which would have ended still more disastrously, had not Palliser come to their assistance, not only with money, but with other efficient help, for he was naturally shrewd in all matters of business, and though ready to spend freely that which he possessed abundantly, he had an instinctive sense of the value of money.

He was very anxious that his sister should spend the winter with her husband, as they had been really, though not ostensibly, separated for the last year, and Palliser had a morbid dread of scandal.

Janet gradually came to understand that Lady Saville had been guilty of some imprudence. What, she did not exactly know, for she was too loyal to ask questions, and too much attached to her sister-in-law to listen to gossip.

As under their circumstances, life was less irksome abroad than in England, Lady Saville decided that Pau would suit them best. Sir Frederic would find golf and hunting, and some of her own more congenial acquaintances intended wintering there. Her eldest boy, to her great delight, had passed for Sandhurst, and Palliser undertook to look after the second, who was at Eton, and invited him to pass Christmas at the Hall.

20*

Lady Saville persuaded Janet to come up to Town to assist her in the rather extensive shopping which was absolutely necessary, she thought, before she went into what she pathetically called banishment, and though Palliser at first objected, he finally yielded to his sister's persuasions.

"After all, shopping is a grand resource," said Lady Saville, one afternoon, as they were sitting at tea in the morning-room or study of the Eaton Square house where they were staying, after a long day, "and a change of occupation and scene is reviving. You were looking awfully moped last week. Tell me, are you quite well? I wish you would confide in me, Janet! Something worries you; there is a subtle change in you. I feel it, though I cannot define it!"

Janet looked up surprised. Lady Saville seldom spoke so seriously, and there was an unusual touch of feeling in her voice.

"Thank you, Gertrude," she returned, roused to sudden caution, for she was determined not to lift the mask. "I feel perfectly

well, and as to being worried, I am sometimes
a little, but with myself. I am, I fancy, wanting in tact and experience, and make mistakes
which——"

"Nonsense, Janet; for a young creature,
brought up like a recluse, you are wonderfully self-possessed. I don't see what mistakes
you make—you are rapidly developing into
a woman of the world! I should greatly
like to give a few hints, a little advice, if you
will not think me taking a liberty, but when
I see you treading the same path I have
stumbled along myself——" She paused.

"Say anything you like," returned Janet
somewhat dejectedly, after waiting for her to
continue.

"How long have you been married?" re-
commenced Lady Saville. "Nearly a year.
Well, you cannot expect a man to be a
lover after twelve months of matrimony,
can you?"

"But I do not expect it, Gertrude. Do I
complain or show dissatisfaction?"

"No, certainly, you are far wiser and more

self-controlled than *I* was! You may not believe it, but I was desperately in love with Sir
Frederic. He was very handsome—at least,
I thought so, and there was something very
taking about him. It lasted a good long
time too—at least with me. He—well, it is
quite different with men, so it was some time
before I found out that I was relegated to the
lumber room of bores. When I *did*, I thought
the world had come to an end, and de-
graded myself with tears and prayers, and
all kinds of useless folly." She laughed.
"Fancy thinking that one could ever touch
the heart of a man who is tired of you!
Why, his heart has ceased to exist for you!
Then I came back to an inferior sort of
existence, and scraped along pretty well.
Now, dear, Randal is a much better man than
Sir Frederic, and I think he had—I mean he
has a better kind of love for you than my
husband had for me; besides, you are a
stronger sort of woman, so he will be longer
fond of you, but do not expect him to continue a lover. It is not in human nature—

cultivate wholesome indifference yourself—
believe me, a man never loves a woman who
is devoted to him as he does one of whom he
is not quite sure. Randal is not unjust. You
will always have all that is due to
your station as his wife, and I prophesy
you will be socially successful. Then
Randal has an infinite horror of gossip. If
he is ever *un peu volage*, it will be in the
most decorous fashion, and you will never
know anything about it!"

Lady Saville had paused more than once
in this long speech, as if to give Janet an
opening, but she did not take advantage of
it. At this last sentence, however, she shrank
as if from a blow.

"Why, Gertrude!" she exclaimed, trying
hard to speak lightly, "what *has* happened
that you should be taken so frightfully prophetic? I do not intend to anticipate im-
probable troubles! I don't wish to impose
lover-like observances on poor Randal (who
so hates to be bored) all the days of his life. I
suppose the transition period is sure to be

more or less unpleasant, but I daresay the loving friendship which succeeds the fancifulness of love is much better, only at first it is rather a come-down. I am sure you are sincerely anxious to help me, but I must take the rough and the smooth as other people do. I do not doubt Randal's sincere affection for a moment."

"You are very brave, I believe, and will manage better than I did," said Lady Saville thoughtfully. "The chief point is not to let your husband see that you cannot exist without him, or you go down twenty per cent. at once."

"I am afraid that Randal has already a shrewd guess at the true state of affairs," returned Janet, smiling.

"Accept another morsel of advice," continued Lady Saville, as if she had not heard her sister-in-law's last words. "If your husband is not sympathetic, don't believe that any other man will be a bit better. They are all alike, only a lover's tenderness will last a little longer than a husband's, because there are a few difficulties in the way, and he holds a freer hand, but they are all alike, and the woman in this case stakes more than the man."

"What an extraordinary opinion you must have of me, Gertrude," began Janet, opening her eyes.

"Oh, yes, I daresay you begin to think I must be a fearfully wicked woman! but I am not; only a very unlucky one. To your untried heart I suppose it seems incredible that anyone should be faithless, even in thought, to a husband. You do not know what it is to hear yourself addressed in tender, respectful accents, when you have been scorned, slighted, and alone! But I do not know what has made me so lugubrious this evening. I wanted to say a word in season, and I suspect I have said too many! I want you, dear, just to put a proper value on your-self—it is quite essential. However, one of these days, when a son and heir appears, you will be mistress of the position, and be sure you take a fast hold of it!"

Before Janet could reply, Lady Saville's

maid, who, with the caretaker and an assistant, formed their temporary staff, came in and announced Lord Darrell.

"Darrell!" cried Lady Saville. "This is delightful. What lucky chance brings you to Town?"

Janet saw, with some surprise, her sister-in-law's sudden and complete change of manner and expression.

"I have just come up from Devonshire, and am on my way to Woodlands. Old Fitzherbert came into the club just now and swore he had seen you and Mrs. Palliser going into some temple of fashion in Regent Street, so I came up here to ascertain the truth," said Darrell, when he had greeted Janet very cordially.

"Now, tell me all about everything," he continued, drawing forward a chair. "No, no tea, thank you, and have you left Palliser lamenting?"

"Not lamenting, I hope," returned Janet. "I have three days' leave of absence to assist Lady Saville in her shopping."

"Do you know we are going to Pau for the winter, Darrell?"

"No, I have heard nothing of you for ages, except that Alec has passed! Well, Pau isn't half a bad place. My uncle will get some hunting. I have half a mind to come and look you up after Christmas. Now tell me, what are you going to do to-night?"

"Nothing but yawn, grumble, and go to bed!" said Lady Saville.

"That will never do. Come and dine with me at the Criterion, and have a look at Wyndham in his new piece."

"It will be charming," cried Lady Saville, quite restored to herself; "would you not like to go, Janet?"

"Very much indeed."

"I must ask you to dine at seven-thirty," said Darrell, "or we cannot see the beginning of the play, which is necessary, I believe. Now I shall go and see if I can find a man or two to join us. This is an unlooked-for pleasure—I will call for you at seven-fifteen— what will Palliser say to such an escapade?"

"That there is safety in a multitude," returned Lady Saville, and she went on to make many enquiries respecting her kinsfolk and acquaintance, which led to some amusing gossip. Then Darrell tore himself away to organize his impromptu dinner, and having written a few lines to Palliser—Janet and her sister-in-law proceeded to make as much of a toilette as their means would allow.

"We are scarcely fit to be seen," said Lady Saville, when they met in the study, which was the only sitting-room prepared for them.

"I suppose we may be looked upon as travellers, and therefore excused all deficiencies. *You* look to me quite ' *en règle.*' "

"To think that half an hour ago we were talking almost tragically, and now we are going off in high glee to enjoy the frivolities of the Criterion!" cried Lady Saville after a brief pause, and she laughed.

" *You* were speaking tragically, Gertrude," returned Mrs. Palliser. "I only listened."

"Well, variability of mood has been my salvation—oh, here is Darrell!"

" Ready ? " said that gentleman coming in in evening dress; " you are miracles of punctuality. Sorry to say I could only secure Monti Douglas and Major Phillips— you know Monti ? Phillips was rather a chum of mine in India, and has only just come back on leave. Come, are you 'fixed up,' as the Yankees say ? "

" Ready—aye, ready ! " said Janet rising, and they were soon on their road to dinner.

There is a kind of special freedom about dinner at a restaurant, a sort of elegant Bohemianism hangs about it, and Mrs. Grundy's grasp is for the moment relaxed. Though she had been startled by Lady Saville's remarks, Janet's deeply - rooted loyalty had taken up arms at once in defence of her husband, and had thus strengthened her own soul. How could Lady Saville for a moment compare that coarse, cynical, unpleasant Sir Frederic to Randal, who was so fastidiously refined ? Randal might have little inequalities of temper—but who was perfect ? She (Janet) had better occupy herself extracting the beams of error which obstructed her own mental vision, than fidget over the motes in her husband's optics. She could not explain why, but this visit to Town, the little change of scene and occupation, seemed to have done her a wonderful amount of good. She felt more like her old light-hearted, fearless self than she had done for many a day. The truth was, she had not to study her words or weigh the tendency of her sentences—what came into her mind she spoke unhesitatingly, and found herself surprisingly fluent.

It was a very pleasant dinner. Monti Douglas was a well-known man about town, the scantily-endowed younger son of a Scotch peer. Major Phillips—a soldier right through, who had been more in India than in London, a good specimen of the kind of man produced by the upper class bourgeoisie. He was greatly amused by the gossip and chaff which was tossed to and fro.

"I hear you mention Langford," he said, as the waiters handed round the dessert; "we have a young fellow from Langford in South-shire in 'ours,' who has just saved the Colonel's life by a lucky shot. His name is Winyard—Maurice Winyard."

"He is the son of our Vicar," returned Janet, deeply interested; "he was a playfellow of mine—I am very glad to hear about him."

"He is a quiet youngster, but he has his wits about him. The Colonel is a curious old chap—he is touched with esoteric Buddhism, whatever that may be, and believes, they say, in lucky stars and lucky men, and a lot more—a regular old fire-eating lion—the men would follow him into the jaws of hell—I beg your pardon."

"Pray don't mind," returned Lady Saville, sweetly. "We have whittled hell down to a mere refined Inferno, nowadays."

Major Phillips stared and laughed.

"At first the Colonel seemed not to notice him, but suddenly he changed — took Winyard out to hunt with him. Just before I started, we had an account from the Hills, where the Colonel and Winyard were having good sport. It seems they had been tracking a man-eating tiger when he turned up suddenly a good bit too near, and sprang on the Colonel; but before he had him on the ground Winyard sent a shot into the beast's ear, so Colonel Drummond got off with a few scratches. The wonder is that Winyard had not winged the Colonel! He must have plenty of nerve and be a capital shot—anyhow, it was a close shave."

"I remember hearing my father say long ago that Maurice was a good shot," replied Janet. "I hope this adventure will prove fortunate to him."

"There is no doubt it will! In spite of his crotchets, the Colonel stands well with the military powers that be."

"I believe Maurice does not suffer from the climate," said Janet.

"No! He had a touch of fever last year, but has been quite right ever since. He was rather silent and moody when he first joined, but he came out wonderfully last winter. Thanks to the commissioner's daughter—a deuced pretty girl, I can tell you!—married General Mackilligan of the ordnance department about three months ago."

"Oh, poor Maurice!" exclaimed Janet, smiling.

"He isn't a penny the worse!" returned Major Phillips. "There are plenty of nice girls everywhere nowadays in India, to keep him going."

"That is a most ambiguous phrase, my dear fellow," cried Darrell. "Do you mean that there are enough pretty girls to keep Mrs. Palliser's interesting young friend going —in flirtation?"

"Well, yes!—it's the best thing for a fellow —and——"

"Ah, they are a bad lot in India evidently," interrupted Darrell; "now, if you will not take any more wine, let us go and see the most fascinating male flirt on the stage."

It had altogether been a very pleasant evening.

Janet found herself smiling over some of the talk and discussions which had gone on, but especially the glimpse of Maurice Winyard's career afforded her by his major's communications, dwelt in her mind. She was sincerely pleased to find that her old friend was making way with his associates. She had been a true prophetess, his fancy for herself had not long borne the heat of the day, yet for all that, she believed Maurice's nature was essentially faithful. How gentle and kindly he was—would he ever be impatient with a wife who tried hard to please him? Yes, of course he would—all men would. "It is their nature." Well, she heartily wished him all possible good fortune and happiness.

Surely it must be a hundred years ago since he came in and found her shelling peas in the kitchen? Was she the same Janet?

Her sister-in-law's absence created a great gap in the Mervyn Hall household, Janet found.

Her knowledge of the world—Palliser's world—was exceedingly useful, and though her nature was slight, it was kindly and specially sympathetic.

Janet was growing more self-distrustful every day, with the result that whenever she hesitated and tried specially hard to do the right thing, the wrong one presented itself and confounded her.

The house had never been quite empty, but the guests had been chiefly gentlemen. Lord Darrell paid a fortnight's visit—Janet always felt she had a backer in him. He made great friends with Captain Rowley also, which was in Janet's favour.

Under cover of this friendship, the old man was more frequently invited to dinner, and matters went with tolerable smoothness.

Darrell protested he would not go home unless Palliser and his wife promised to come to Woodlands for a week or ten days.

"You have the best preserves, Palliser," he said, "but you'll find our Yorkshire hunting first rate. I wish you had not put your spoke in your wife's hunting tendencies. She would have been ready to come out with us by this time if you had let her ride all the summer."

21*

"I assure you I have no wish to interfere. Mrs. Palliser can do as she likes."

"Thank you," said Janet.

"That is all very fine, Palliser, but you have killed the wish."

"Never mind," added Janet, "I am always greatly amused to drive to the meet in my humble pony-carriage, and I shall be equally gratified to see you 'off' at Woodlands."

"You are considerably too angelic, Mrs. Palliser! Now, am I to see you on the seventh or eighth of December? I'll try and get a jolly party together. I fear most of the best people are engaged."

"If you have good hunting, that is the great point."

"Thank you, Lord Darrell. I shall be very pleased."

And this was true, she was beginning to be just a little afraid of a *tête-à-tête* with her husband. It gave him such ample room for fault-finding.

This invitation would fill up the time pleasantly till Christmas. Then Lady Saville's

youngest boy was to come to Mervyn; Mary
Winyard and her husband were to be at the
Vicarage, and Randal would give them a
dinner. Then they were to have a tenants'
ball, and a ball for the gentry—tremendous
projects which would have had no terrors
whatever for Janet, could she have felt sure
of pleasing her husband, or secure of not
displeasing him. But her whole life was an
uncertainty.

"Did you get wet?" asked Palliser, one
afternoon about two days before they were
to start for Yorkshire, as she came into the
drawing-room, her cheeks glowing from her
race with the rain. Her dark grey eyes
deepened into blue. She removed her hat,
and pushed her wavy braids of hair from her
brow.

"No, I just escaped, but I had to run for
it."

She stood by the table, and poured out a
cup of tea which she brought to him.

Palliser rose from his easy chair, took it
from her and placed it on the mantel-piece.

"Janet," he said, drawing her to him, and looking down into her face with admiring eyes. "After all you are very sweet. And a deuced deal handsomer than when I first fell in love with you. I wish——"

He paused, and then kissed her brow and lips.

"What do you wish, dear Randal?" she whispered softly, while her heart beat to suffocation. Was she on the point of learning the word of the riddle? "Why do you not tell me? All *I* wish is to make you happy!"

"There are so many little things—that—you don't seem to understand—you do not exactly feel with me. I am rather sensitive, and I wish you could divine my wishes!"

Janet looked at him with distressed, wistful eyes.

"I fear I am dull, dear. Oh, that I had a spirit of divination! but as it is wanting, do tell me what my deficiencies are! I know so well when you are dissatisfied, which, alas! is very often, and I am *so* miserable because

I don't know why.   If you only knew *how* miserable I am sometimes, you would be sorry."

The soft, loving arms went up round his neck, her sweet fresh lips clung to his, and as she felt how passionately he returned her kisses, a flood of sunshine seemed to fill her heart with intoxicating delight.   All troubles and misunderstandings must be at an end. He would open his heart to her, and show her how to please and satisfy him, and she would find it to be the omission or commission of some mere trifle which she had been too dense to perceive.

"Now do tell me what are my special stupidities."

"I don't know that it is worth while talking about it just now.   I am, perhaps, a little impatient, and—but there, don't let us waste these precious moments on disagreeable things.   In less than an hour we must dress for that infernal dinner at the Beauchamps'.   Come, and sit down beside me, and let us talk of my plans.   I had a

letter from Compton ·this morning—(he is
the Conservative Whip, you know.) He says
our old representative Digby is going to
retire from public life. He is quite sure of it.
It will be announced after Christmas, then
we'll have a busy time of it, Janet! I shall
have my manifesto ready to post, directly
Digby's good - bye to the constituency is
published. I shall see Godfrey on my way
through Town. I mean the agent—he is a
first-rate man.   I think I am tolerably
popular in the county, even with the bump-
kins, eh ? "

"I am sure you are, Randal!" said Janet,
speaking her real conviction, and perceiving
that this was not the time to press for any
rules whereby to guide her conduct, as the
greater had completely swallowed up the
lesser, in Palliser's mind. So she gave her
whole attention to electioneering schemes,
until the dressing-bell summoned them—
somewhat earlier than usual—as they had a
six-mile drive to their dinner-party.

" What are you going to wear, Janet ? "

" Green velvet, I think ! "

" No, put on your white gown with the lace concern over your shoulders."

" Very well," said Janet, laughing, " I am not sure that Raynes will be pleased if she has put out the velvet."

" Well, you must face her wrath for my sake ! "

" In such a cause I will not hesitate," said his wife, as she left the room.

The dinner was more amusing than Palliser expected, and everyone observed how brilliantly well Mrs. Palliser was looking. This was as it should be, he thought. It was her bounden duty to do credit to his choice.

There was some gossip about the county member, and a report that he thought of retiring was mentioned. Of course, Palliser held his tongue respecting the information he had received, but he was a little ruffled because nobody said anything about his being a fit and proper person to represent the county in Parliament.

He was amiable enough on the following

morning, but could talk of nothing except the coming election, but seemed to be pleased to have a listener in his wife.

The next day but one they were to start for Lord Darrell's place, breaking their journey in London—as it was rather long—and Palliser wanted to see his agent.

They were not to leave till after luncheon, for Palliser's appointment was not till the following morning.

Janet was looking forward to her visit with a good deal of pleasure. She liked Lord Darrell, and knew several of the guests he had invited. She hoped, too, that she should be successful in steering clear of all rocks of offence, for she fancied she had discovered one or two trifling causes of irritation, so trifling that she could have laughed, had they not affected Randal.

"I think it will be a fine day," said Palliser when he sat down to breakfast; "it is rather a fine line of country up to Woodlands, but flat when you get there. However, it well be dark by the time we arrive to-morrow."

" What letters have you ? "

" A long one from Gertrude—she seems better pleased with Pau than she expected, but they have not had a good winter—as to weather."

Having appeased the pangs of hunger, Palliser took up *The Times*, throwing the advertisement sheet — after the fashion of Creation's lords — on the carpet, while he scanned the paper for some mention of Mr. Digby's retirement.

An exclamation from Janet attracted his attention—she was evidently reading the first column, the famous list of births, deaths, and marriages.

" Oh, Randal ! just think, Richard Palliser has a little son ! 'On the fifth instant, at St. Oswald's, Sussex, the wife of R. Palliser, Esq. of a son and heir.' "

" What ! " exclaimed Palliser in a tone that startled his wife.

" There it is," she said, offering it to him, and feeling suddenly as if something tragic had happened.

"Don't show it to me!" said he, rising and throwing away his part of the paper. "No! give it to me!" he snatched, rather than took it from her hand.

"Insolent scoundrel!" as he glanced at the announcement, and crushed the unoffending print in his grasp. "What does he mean by 'son and *heir*?' Heir to Mervyn?—not yet, Mr. Richard Palliser, not yet!" and he began to pace the room.

Janet felt stunned and utterly at a loss what to say, so wisely kept silence, the colour gradually fading from her face, as she recalled Lady Saville's sentence, "When a son and heir appears, you will be mistress of the position." Was this the secret of her failure to be all she ought to be? How was it that her husband was so eager to have a son to inherit his lands, his name? It was a sort of prospective greediness she could not quite understand, and yet it was common enough, natural enough, she supposed.

But how unjust to visit such a sin of omission on her head, when she would so gladly have welcomed a baby—boy or girl.

What could she say?—was the question that racked both brain and heart—she could find no answer.

Meantime Palliser paced the room utterly regardless of his wife's growing pallor, half wild with anger and envy.

"Those infernal money grubbers have all the luck!" he exclaimed at length. "When I made the great mistake of my life, that shopkeeping wife of Dick Palliser's took it for granted her husband or her son would be the head of the family—she will begin to believe it again!"

Still Janet could not speak, a strange struggle between a sense of guilt and a sense of injustice was going on in her heart, and no words would come. At last she faltered, "How do you know that Mrs. Richard thought such things?" was the unfortunate observation.

"For God's sake don't argue," cried Palliser roughly; "you know nothing about it, and care less!" And he resumed his walk.

Janet was struck dumb. She sat still for a minute or two, then she took up the paper, folded and laid it on the table, and was gently leaving the room, when her movement caught Palliser's notice.

"Where are you going?" he asked, "to hide your ill-temper, because I cannot always conceal my disappointment and annoyance! You ought to have more sympathy with me!"

"I have all possible sympathy with you, Randal, and I have no ill-temper to hide. I was going away because you are not yourself, and you are speaking more unkindly than you know. You will be sorry afterwards, so it is better not to stay here now," and she left the room.

When she reached her own, she sat down like one stunned, she felt no inclination to shed tears.

A curious sort of chill numbed her from head to foot. She felt as if she had been turned on the world in the cold. What right

had she to be where she was?—she had not
fulfilled the ends of her existence! What
business had she to pose as the mistress of
Mervyn Hall, deficient as she was in her
principal duty? She felt like a swindler,
who ought to be banished from the paradise
she had entered on false pretences! A
feeling of black despair wrapped her in the
dull muffling of its dismal atmosphere.

"I beg your pardon, madam," said Raynes,
who came quickly into the room on packing
bent, and started back, greatly surprised to
see her lady there at that hour.

"Do not mind, Raynes, go on with your
packing," she brought out the words with
difficulty.

"I beg your pardon, ma'am, but are you
feeling unwell?"

"Not quite as well as usual," returned her
mistress, trying to smile. "I must go out—
the air will revive me."

"Won't you lie down and rest, ma'am?
It's bad to travel when one is not quite right;
shall I fetch you some sal volatile?"

"No, thank you. I am almost myself again. I will go and see if Mr. Palliser is going out." She rose and left the room, pausing in the next one, to think what she should do. Was Randal waiting to ask her forgiveness for his outbreak? He ought to follow her for that purpose, but she would not exact too much, nor would she be inexorable, but she would tell him how cruelly he had hurt her, and yet it was a bitter annoyance, this birth of a son to his cousin. She knew him (Randal) better than she used —and——How unfortunate she was! She began to understand that her husband did not easily forgive failure, or contradiction, still he would be sorry for having spoken as he did, and she must make him understand that although grieved, she was not in a bad temper. Thank Heaven, she had resisted tears. If only she looked less pale!—a quick walk round the garden might remedy that. She dreaded meeting Randal again, but that was silly! He would say a few apologetic words, and promise "not to do it again," then all

would be over, only—she could never forget
—never!

She gathered up her forces and descended
to the library. Palliser was writing, and as
Janet crossed the room, she saw that the evil
spirit still reigned within him. His smile
was exceedingly pleasant, but when it was
not playing round his lips or laughing in his
eyes, the master of Mervyn looked a very
ugly customer indeed.

"Oh, is that you? I wish you would write
a line for me to Godfrey; say I cannot see
him till twelve instead of eleven to-morrow.
I have a telegram from Compton—he wants
me to be with him as early as I can, so we cannot get off to Woodlands by the mid-day train.
I told Cootes to look out and arrange for the
next. No; take my paper, yours is too small
and finikin; use the third person, you know."

And this was all. He seemed to have no
consciousness of needing pardon; he held
himself as if he were the offended party. She
need not have feared a melting appeal for pardon, or planned her own phrases in reply, so

trivial a matter as her sorely-wounded heart did not cost him a second thought. She drew the paper towards her and began to write, but she could not command her attention, and she had to re-write it twice.

When, at last, it was accomplished, she handed it to her husband, asking, "Would you like to look at it?"

He glanced at her and the torn pieces of paper.

"I hope to Heaven, Janet, you are not going in for nerves!" he said with a frown. "You are looking like a ghost! I thought you had the nerves and health of a milkmaid!"

"If my nerves were shaken for a moment, you have quite restored them," she said steadily. "They shall not trouble you again."

"I am glad to hear it; I should be awfully disgusted if you treated us to hysterics at Darrell's place."

His tone roused the stout spirit that underlay Janet's loving nature, and she pulled herself together without much effort.

"Very well," she said. "And *I* shall be

greatly disgusted if you break your leg or
arm while we are at Lord Darrell's.   If you
do, don't expect me to nurse you, so take care."

There was a certain lightness in her tone
which startled him, not a tinge of ill-temper,
but a touch of good-humoured defiance.
Palliser looked at her for a moment—a change,
not to softness, passing over his face.

"I hope I shall not trouble you.   Will
you stamp these letters?   I am going to ride
into the post myself.   I'll be back in time for
lunch."

Then Janet hastily wrapped herself up and
rushed away into the woods.   Was it possible
that her husband, who could be so charming,
so loving, was merely heartless—sounding
brass?   Had she been conscious of treating
him with cruel indifference, would any atone-
ment seem sufficient?   Could anything ever
heal this cruel wound?   How thankful she
would be to forget it!   Perhaps as time went
on, she would grow harder, wiser, more fit
for general circulation, better able to estimate
things, and then, would life be worth living?

22*

CHAPTER III.

A WINTRY SUN.

The journey to London seemed long and dreary. Palliser had not got over his bad temper. He was not cross. He was preoccupied and utterly oblivious of having behaved unfeelingly. Janet's pride helped her to keep up a brave show. They even spoke occasionally on indifferent topics. When dinner was over Palliser rose and lit a cigar.

"It is so dreadfully dull here," he said. "I think I'll look in at one of the theatres. There is something rather good going on at the Vaudeville. I daresay you will be glad to get to bed, as you have a journey before you."

That day left an indelible stamp upon Janet's heart, for she felt that it was the beginning of troubles.

Of course, Randal was in a very bad temper, and, later on, might be sorry, but she began to doubt if he would ever say so. Even if pride—which she could not help feeling was extremely petty, kept him from saying in so many words that he regretted having hurt her, he might show by his manner, his acts, that he wished to be all right with her again, she would, of course, give him plenary absolution, yet if he had frequent attacks of this kind, could she go on always forgiving? Pray God that she might always love him tenderly. To lose her own love would be even worse than losing his. That would be the abomination of desolation indeed! But she was growing quite morbid, all this bitterness would blow over. She would take some opportunity when Randal was in a happy mood, and ask him if he realised the pain he had given her. It was rather silly to have to wait till a creature, supposed to be stronger and wiser than herself, was in a rational mood, in order to put a self-evident proposition before him. "But

we are all weak and foolish sometimes, I
suppose."

With this safe generalisation she fell asleep,
quite worn out by the emotions of the day.

Next morning was dull and drizzling, but
Janet was determined not to sit indoors and
mope, so sent for a cab, and drove away with
the serious Mrs. Raynes to gather what pleasure
she could from the South Kensington Museum.
But she found it a little difficult to fix her
attention on the various artistic objects which
she tried to explain to her companion, who
observed:

" Well, 'm, I don't know that people need
go so much abroad, I'm sure I never knew
there were such a heap of beautiful things
in London."

The journey to Woodlands was a trifle less
dreary than the previous day's. Palliser was
a good deal taken up with his newspaper and
some notes he had brought with him from his
interview with the Conservative whip. He
seemed in fairly good humour, and spoke
occasionally to his wife, rather as if to him-

self than consciously to another. She listened with due interest, and so long as she could see, solaced herself with a thrilling romance picked up at the terminus.

Lord Darrell himself awaited them on their arrival.

His warm welcome was quite charming to Janet after the awful gloom of the last two days. He was so unaffectedly pleased to see her that she could have given him a sisterly pat on the shoulder.

" It's so good of you, Mrs. Palliser, to come all this way to a disconsolate bachelor. I have persuaded my mother to come and do the honours for me ; she has not had the pleasure of meeting you, but I fancy you will like her."

" I shall be delighted to make her acquaintance," returned Janet. " I have often heard how charming she is."

" Well, she has lived every hour of her life, and is still young. We have Major Phillips with us for a few days, and he is looking forward to renewing his acquaintance with you."

Then he asked for news of the Savilles.
Palliser replied and the four or five miles
between the station and the house were got
over quickly.

Woodlands was intensely modern, but
luxurious in its appointments and richly
furnished, still Janet recognised the superior
stateliness of Mervyn Hall.

A whole train of servants were ready to
receive them, and they were at once ushered
into the library, where the Dowager awaited
her guests. A tall, stately woman, rather
stout, but by no means shapeless, with a fine,
intelligent face, not handsome, but strong and
pleasant, surmounted by a quantity of silvery-
grey hair, turned back in the style that used
to be called *à l'Impératrice,* over which lay a
kerchief of fine lace, and was clad in a long,
trailing tea - gown of rich black brocade.
Such was the figure that came forward to
greet Janet with high-bred ease and kindly
frankness.

"You look cold and tired, my dear Mrs.
Palliser! I ordered your tea to be served in

your dressing-room—it still wants an hour and a half to dinner, so you will have time to rest; most of the men are out—they went to rather a distant meet, but they ought to be back soon. Very glad to see you, Mr. Palliser; it is a long time since we met—nearly six years ago in Rome. Fortune has favoured you since!" with a quick, smiling glance at his wife. " Darrell, I leave Mr. Palliser to you, while I take Madame to her room."

" Pray, do not trouble yourself," began Janet.

" It is no trouble. I am quite a young woman in some ways."

" One of the most energetic of young women!" said Lord Darrell laughing, and evidently proud of his mother. " You need not fear my mother's over-fatiguing herself, Mrs. Palliser — she is ready for everything from pitch-and-toss to manslaughter ! "

" What a character from one's only boy ! Come then, Mrs. Palliser."

She led the way through a long corridor,

deliciously warmed, to a grand staircase, ascending which they reached the dressing-room, where Raynes had already begun to unpack.

"Oh, tea is in your bedroom! *Tant mieux*. Your maid can go on with her un-packing. Take off your outdoor things—it will rest you. Draw that chair for your mistress."

Lady Darrell subsided into another, and proceeded to pour out tea, and hand the delicate "tartines" to Janet.

"I think you know my brother, Sir Frederic Saville," said Lady Darrell, setting to work on a huge, homely-looking piece of knitting, which was tucked under her arm. "I have heard my nephew, Alec, talk of Mervyn Hall as an earthly paradise, and of you as its presiding goddess."

"That is because Mr. Palliser and myself are fond of him. He is such a nice boy!"

"Yes, he is like his mother, and she is very attractive both to men and women, which is unusual — generally, those who attract the one repel the other! I heard of you in Rome, too. You knew the Beauchamps, didn't you?—they are your neighbours at Mervyn."

"Yes, we see them often."

"I am glad I happened to be in England just now," continued Lady Darrell, "and could come to meet you. Generally, I have flown south with the swallows before this time of the year. I hate winter in England— I like the freedom of the Continent—that is, the freedom English people have there, for the natives are fettered from the cradle to the grave. Now I shall leave you to rest. You will hear the dressing bell in good time ; we are a very small party this evening, but some neighbours are coming to dinner who are rather interesting," and Lady Darrell sailed away.

Janet was thankful for the complete change, and was immensely attracted by her host's mother. She wished she dared take counsel with such a woman ; her experience would make her advice worth having, but even to a mother, she ought not to speak too confidentially of a husband's little infirmities of temper.

Dinner passed over pleasantly, and Janet enjoyed a long talk with Major Phillips about India and Maurice Winyard. The neighbours proved to be very musical, and Janet was of some use in playing one or two accompaniments to the duets of the two sisters, who, with their father, were the guests from the neighbourhood.

Janet thought herself especially fortunate in being very much with Lady Darrell, who was greatly taken with her young guest. The other ladies—a gay widow and a very fast young married woman—"walked with the guns," and even brought down their birds occasionally, followed the hounds, and looked with indulgent contempt on Janet as a poor submissive creature, whose grovelling nature disposed her to bear uncomplainingly a husband's tyranny.

"You are a wonderful person, my dear Mrs. Palliser!" said Lady Darrell one

morning, when her son had come in to speak
of the day's plans before starting for the meet.

'You do not hunt, nor shoot, nor smoke, nor
—yes—you play billiards very well, I believe,
so you are are obliged to put up with an old
woman's company. I fear——"

"No, dear Lady Darrell, you cannot fear
that I am dull," interrupted Janet. "I am
most happy and amused with you. The days
seem short and are only running away too
swiftly! I have always been accustomed
to be quiet; our walks and drives are
delightful."

"You are a charming flatterer," said her
hostess laughing.

"But I have learned a secret," said Darrell,
who was buttoning his glove, with his hunting
crop under his arm. "Mrs. Palliser has the
greatest wish to ride, and her ferocious
spouse, for some reason or other, will not
let her! Look here, Mrs. Palliser, I have
an ideal lady's horse, and to-morrow they
are all going to the meet at the Miller's
copse. I'll stay at home, and you and I will

have a quiet canter round the roads, if it's
a fine day as it promises to be, for the
weather seems settled."

" Many thanks, Lord Darrell, though
perhaps I ought to scold you for tempting
me. However, I cannot yield, for I have
not brought my habit."

" Too bad of you, Mrs. Palliser! I can
only repeat my warning—you'll ruin your
husband. Couldn't you send for your
habit ? "

" No, it is of no use," said Janet, shaking
her head. "I will not ride, unless Randal
comes with me."

" Did you ever hear anything like it ? "
said Lord Darrell to his mother. " Well, I
shall be late, so good-bye for the present. I
am awfully vexed with you, Mrs. Palliser."

" Do you think me very silly ? " asked
Janet, who longed to open her heart to her
kind hostess.

" No, my dear Mrs. Palliser, no one can
judge fairly without full knowledge, and that
I do not possess. You may be acting with

sound judgment—I am a strong advocate for upholding one's rights, yet it is often true wisdom to give in gracefully ; you ought to know your husband better than anyone else, and must feel what would please or annoy him. I don't think anyone can advise a wife."

" No, I suppose not," said Janet thoughtfully ; " besides, it would give me no pleasure to ride when I know it would displease my husband."

" The best of men have fits of unreason," said Lady Darrell philosophically. " But warm love is the best solvent of all difficulties— where that exists everything will come right."

Janet was silent. A pang shot through her heart, for she no longer felt that heavenly security which made life too blissful. Some association of ideas with the first fair summer days of her home-coming prompted the question.

" You have been at Mervyn, I think, Lady Darrell ? "

" Yes, a long time ago, when my brother

was engaged to Gertrude. Mr. Palliser's mother was alive then (you know your husband had a long minority). It is a sweet place, perhaps a little buried in woods, but the house is lovely."

"It is! I remember what a grand place I thought it when I was a little girl, and I used to ramble about the woods with my father. I fancied Mr. Palliser must be a sort of prince. He was hardly ever at Mervyn then. It was very extraordinary that I should be his wife after all."

"Not so very extraordinary," said Lady Darrell, smiling. "We were all very pleased to hear that Mr. Palliser had made a nice happy marriage. I believe I am rather a worldly woman, but I have a little faith left in affection, only those capable of feeling it are few and far between."

Janet was always pleased to listen when Lady Darrell spoke. She had seen much, with shrewd, observant eyes, and her generalisations were keen and broad. Considered worldly among the worldly, she had hidden deep down in her heart a golden vein of pity and tenderness, which she rarely displayed. Though always holding her place in society with dignity, she was a strict economist, and it was rumoured had scraped together a large amount of property. She loved dabbling in the money market, and was supposed to be lucky in her speculations, but she never communicated her affairs to anyone. Once when her son, of whom she was extremely fond, had dipped himself by his extravagance, she came to his assistance with an amount which surprised him. But she was very particular as to the securing of the sum advanced on mortgage, and the regular payment of interest.

Janet was surprised to find how much Lady Darrell read, all kinds of books, tough and dry, poetry, history, even light society novels, she seemed to have skimmed the cream of all, besides being fairly familiar with French and Italian literature.

" How do you find time for it all ? " asked Janet.

"We always find time for what we like," she returned. "By-and-bye, when Mr. Palliser goes into political life, as I hope he will—you will have much more time to yourself, and then I fancy you will be a voracious reader. It is almost the only inexhaustible pleasure. But when you go regularly to Town, and gather a social circle round you, you will be carried away from books for a while, yet I fancy you will return to them, the taste for reading is in you."

"I am very fond of people too," said Janet. "They interest me immensely."

"So much the better! Don't *show* too much difference from your neighbours, people resent eccentricity."

"There is a very good library at the Hall. I do hope, dear Lady Darrell, you will come and stay with us!"

"I shall be very pleased, when I return to England, but I intend to be at Pau for Christmas. I have promised my brother and Lady Saville. Now I have letters to write, and you?"

" So have I! I like to send my dear father long letters, they amuse him."

" No doubt. The absent are apt to fancy themselves forgotten."

Janet never knew if Palliser was aware of her refusal to ride. As he seemed more cordial and talkative on the rare occasions when they were alone together, she hoped he was, but she had now begun to think before she spoke to him, to turn subjects over before she ventured to broach them, and the result was that she felt mentally in irons. She longed unspeakably to tear away the veil which seemed to hide them from each other—but how was she to do it? If she could find a favourable moment, and gently reproach him for his coldness, ever since he had heard of the arrival of his cousin's son and heir, he might be touched and assure her of his love. She must not be a coward, there was no cause whatever why she should not speak to her husband on that, or any other subject.

Their visit to Woodlands was drawing to

23*

an end. It had been very successful, Palliser was occupied and amused, and Janet was a general favourite.

The evening but two before they were to leave, a certain Lord Alan Seymour, an exceedingly critical personage, of the highest fashion, whose dictum on beauty and art, the drama and literature, was considered among a certain set, final, arrived for a day or two on his way to some ducal mansion in Scotland. He was immensely attracted by Janet, who was quite unmoved by his admiration, and equally ignorant of his high reputation; she therefore talked to him as easily and naturally as if he were one of the Saville boys. Lord Alan was refreshed and amused, and confided to Lord Darrell that he had not met so charming a woman for many a day. Janet's spirits rose, feeling that she had made a little success. It would be a sort of backing up for her intended attempt at explanation and the recurrence to the old confidential tone which had existed between them.

When she reached her dressing-room that

evening, she told her maid she would ring when she wanted her, and taking a book, sat down by the fire to wait for her husband. He did not come for a considerable time, but when she heard his step in his dressing-room she went to meet him.

He looked a little surprised.

"Up still?" he said.

"Yes, I want to talk to you, Randal."

"Have you any terrible confession to make?" he asked smiling. "Has Seymour been making love to you?—he seemed rather smitten."

"Nonsense, Randal! I am a great goose, dear, but I am nervous about saying what I have to say!" she slipped her arm through his arm and pressed it to her.

"You ought to wear that pearl necklace oftener," he said, looking down at her white throat critically, "it suits you better than diamonds! Why don't you have your dresses cut like Mrs. Vereker's?"

"Randal! would you like me to wear my dress like *hers!*"

" Well, not *quite* so low perhaps, but pray do not be a prude ! Now then, what is it ? " passing his arm lightly round her.

This was promising. He was in a good mood.

" Don't you think you were a bad boy to speak to me so harshly ? "

" Harshly—when ? " his brow clouding over.

" That morning—the day we left Mervyn, when you were so cross." Palliser drew away his arm, and disengaged the other from her hold, but gently.

" If you were wise," he said coldly, " you would make no allusion to that unfortunate morning ! I was. a good deal moved, and naturally, but I do not think I said anything I need regret. I wonder I had so much self-control, especially as you were utterly silent and immovable ; *that* provoked me more than anything else, let me hear no more on the subject—let me forget ! it is your best plan ! "

Janet stood stunned and speechless, she was so strangely put in the wrong, the tone of

her husband's mind was so absolutely in
discord with her own, that the folly of
attempting explanation or remonstance
flashed upon her with overwhelming conviction. It was over, all hope in that
direction. But she pulled herself together
for one more effort. She would not submit
to a charge of indifference, she drew a little
further away and said gently but firmly,
" You misunderstood me, Randal!—whatever
distresses you is also grief to me! you will
come to know this."

" I am quite willing to believe it," he
returned with the same air of lofty superiority
—" I beg the matter may be dropped."

" Certainly it shall be," replied Janet. " I
will never speak of it again," and seeing that
Palliser laid his hand on the bell, to summon
his valet, she turned and left the room.

Yes!—it was quite finished, that passage
which she thought she might have turned to
good account, and touched his heart by
showing the power he possessed to wound
hers. She would never offend him again,

nor should she ever again be able to speak
to him with frankness and trust as she used.
She would do her best to be good and loving,
but they never again could be as they once
were—some charm had evaporated, some
link had snapped.

The remainder of their visit was as
successful as the beginning had been, and
Lord Alan Seymour was quite openly devoted
to Mrs. Palliser to the last, escorting her to
the station, and expressing ardent hopes of
seeing her in Town in the spring.

Lord Darrell promised to " look them up "
at Mervyn after Christmas, and his mother
kissed the young guest at parting with more
warmth than she had shown any one for
years.

CHAPTER IV.

CHRISTMAS and its festivities were scarcely past and everyone was still in full cry respecting the brilliancy and agreeability of the Mervyn Hall entertainments.

Janet had enjoyed them herself—she loved music and dancing, and on the whole Palliser seemed well pleased — she was also glad to see her old friend Mary looking well and happy, to make her husband's acquaintance, and see an increasing glow of peaceful sunset in the dear old vicarage, where the struggle for life had been hard enough.

People were beginning to talk of the coming session, and the various measures likely to be brought forward, when one morning at breakfast (the usual time for important announcements) Palliser looked up

from his letters with an animated expression
and exclaimed :

" Well, it is an accomplished fact at last !
—old Digby has resigned. I suppose his
valedictory address to his constituents will
be in to-morrow's *Courant*."

" I am so glad he has retired instead of
dying ! " cried Janet, her face lighting up in
sympathy ; " now you must set to work at
once to canvass."

" I must telegraph to Godfrey," said
Palliser, rising to ring the bell, " he promised
to be my secretary *pro tem.*—you will order
them to have a room prepared for him. He
can write in my study — fortunately my
manifesto is quite ready."

" If *I* can help in any writing, pray
employ me, Randal."

" Thank you, yes. Bring me a telegraph
form and an envelope," he continued to the
servant who obeyed the bell. " I want one of
the men to take this at once to the post
office."

" I should like to read your manifesto, or

whatever it is," said Janet; "have you a copy?"

"Yes, plenty of copies; fortunately I took time by the forelock—I don't think you will understand much about it."

Janet smiled.

"At least I can try!" she said.

Palliser looked at her as if he had been scarcely aware of her before.

"For Heaven's sake, whatever fad you take up, don't besmirch yourself with politics. Women become pitiable objects when they try to handle what is beyond their grasp."

"Very well!" she returned, genuinely amused at his horror. "I promise never to worry you or any one else about the forbidden topic — but I suppose I may read your speeches in the privacy of my own chamber."

"You may read anything in the world you like! Now I will write a few letters, then I'll ride over to B——. I must see the editor of the *Southshire Courant*, and persuade him to make room for *my* address too, in to-morrow's edition. That little

bumptious dissenter Canton, whose h's are
so inextricably confused, will have *his* out by
to-morrow, I imagine. How the *Langford
Mercury* will 'blackguard' poor old Digby,
and myself."

"I might drive you over to B—— in the
pony carriage!" exclaimed Janet. "I am
quite eager to be up and doing something."

"Pray adopt a masterly system of inaction,"
said Palliser impressively. "I am most anxious
to keep you out of the mire," and gathering
up his papers he went away to the library.

"It will be an exciting time," thought Janet.
"I wish he would let me be a little in it. It
may be only an ignorant interest, but I *am*
very deeply interested—at any rate, I can
read up everything. I do hope he will win.
I cannot bear to think of his being disappointed or mortified, and certainly it will be
worse for everyone round if he is."

Janet, after a few moments' thought, determined not to write to anyone until she had
heard from her husband what he wished or
did not wish her to say—though she was

anxious to answer an interesting and amusing letter she had had from Lady Darrell—and being unable to settle either to book or work, she set forth to pay a visit to her father—to him she knew she could speak with safety.

It always strengthened and revived her to be in the open air, and for the last month or six weeks, her great object was to avoid loneliness and thought. She sought by all possible means to keep up her strength, her hope—she felt she was going through a dark passage, in which, could she have found a light, it might perhaps have shown her ghastly things. So she clung desperately to the friendly gloom, holding on desperately to her own love for, and belief in, Palliser, feeling that if that were wrenched from her, it would be shipwreck indeed.

It was a great excitement for Captain Rowley, and his daughter rejoiced to see how he brightened up under the stir and impetus of public interest centred round one so nearly connected with him. Janet had thought him a little dull and quiet of late, but now he was himself again and made himself quite useful to Palliser's agent by his knowledge of the Langford people, their interests and opinions. In short, everything was merged in the contest, which was the more exciting, as the Liberals and Radicals offered a strong opposition to the Conservative candidate. Things were hurried on, too, that the new member might take his seat on the reassembling of Parliament.

To Janet it was all very exciting, and though strictly obedient to her husband's command " not to meddle," she made herself mistress of every detail, and sometimes managed a little talk with the secretary, who often gave her the key to the puzzle when she was mystified.

It was a sort of revelation to her, and did not elevate politics in her eyes. Still, the contest interested her intensely, and quite accounted to her for being absolutely over-looked by Palliser. How could he think of anything save his speeches and the manœuvres of his agents? He did not

speak badly either. He had carefully got
up all the subjects he had intended to handle,
and his profound pride, his deep conviction
of his superiority to the vulgar herd whom
he addressed, gave him an air of certainty
and command, which was very effective.

At last the struggle culminated in a very
fair majority for Palliser, and the eating, the
health drinking, the speechifying, the congratulations, the assurances that the country
was saved once more, were all over, and for
a few days Palliser and his wife took breath.

It was not for long.

"If you want to come up to Town with
me," he said one day after dinner, " you had
better let me know, for we must see about a
house."

"Want to go up to Town with you?"
repeated Janet, feeling almost dazed by the
question. "Why? Do you wish me to
stay here?"

"Pray do not invent grievances. I only
want you to do what you like. Of course
you will come up after Easter, but just now,

at the beginning of things, it will be dull,
and I shall run down from Friday to Monday
whenever I can."

Janet hesitated. She earnestly desired to
do the right thing, if only she knew which it
was. For a moment she hesitated as to what
she wished.

"Dear Randal," she exclaimed, "do tell
me what *you* would wish. I am quite
content to do as you like."

"No, no. I really cannot make up your
mind for you. You are a responsible being,
decide for yourself."

"Does he wish me to stay here?" thought
Janet, greatly racked by her own uncertainty.
"As I must choose," was her final decision,
"I shall choose what I like."

"Well, Randal," she said, "I am dying
to hear you speak on the address, and of
course I should prefer in any case being with
you."

"Thank you," he said, not effusively.
"Very nice of you, I am sure," and he helped
himself to claret.

Janet's heart throbbed to bursting, and never did she accomplish anything more heroic than holding back the tears which almost forced themselves into her eyes. She felt she had chosen, not the better part, not the part she was intended to choose, and now she could not change without making too much ado, or seeming slavish in her readiness.

What her husband evidently meant was that she should divine his wishes and utter them as her own. As it was, she must not draw back. Was it possible he wished to go to Town *without* her? Was *she*, too, becoming a bore? No, she would not think of it. She would not—could not accept such a terrible interpretation of his manner, more than his words. But he was speaking again in a quiet matter of fact way.

"I think, then, the best thing I can do is to take the Savilles' house for the season, furnished as it is; before our time is up, I shall know if it is a desirable abode, and take a lease of it, buying up the furniture, which will want to be very considerably renewed."

" Yes, that seems the best plan," said Janet, not too steadily.

"I am afraid," resumed Palliser, looking at her with the peculiarly keen look he had when not quite pleased, and which seemed to draw his eyes closer together. "I am afraid you will develop a furious taste for gaiety and frivolity! I observe whenever you and I are left together after a spell of racket, you become tearful, with or without reason."

"Indeed—indeed you mistake me, Randal," cried Janet, yielding to the impulse of her candid nature. "I am quite happy with you—but, the truth is, I was silly enough to fear, from your tone, that you—that you began to find me a bore," and she managed a little laugh which some men might have found pathethic.

"I am not aware that I was so ill-bred as to give you that impression. It is quite erroneous! I thought you were a sensible and indeed a strong-minded woman. This

kind of sensitive weakness is exceedingly
destructive to peace and comfort ; pray
regulate your fancies, for in the intimacy of
everyday life, it is rather a nuisance to stop
and pick one's words, lest they should unlock
the flood-gates !"

"I assure you you need have no such
dread, Randal," her voice was quite steady
now. "I am not a crying character. Yes, as
you were saying, the Savilles' house would
suit us very well. I shall probably write to
Gertrude to-morrow. Shall I mention the
matter to her?"

"No, no! Never transact business with
a relative personally if possible. My man of
business shall write to Saville. We shall
not want all the servants till after Easter, but
you will settle that with Mrs. Dunford. You
seem to be rather bright about household
matters."

"Only lately then," returned his wife.
"At first, after our tiny cottage and one
servant, this establishment seemed appalling."

They talked on, with increasing composure

24*

on Janet's part. She was beginning to perceive that neither emotion, nor tenderness, nor anything, suited Randal unless he took the initiative himself, and for the first time a sense of impatient weariness began to steal over her, at the prospect of always waiting for his lead, instead of following her own impulse, in showing her taste, her fancies, above all, her affection to him.

She said she was tired, and bid him good-night a little earlier than usual.

Palliser sat on musing over the papers, which he now read with the closest attention, while he solaced himself with a fragrant cigarette. He was in a placid frame of mind —he gave some complacent thoughts to his wife.

" Of course I made rather a fool of her at first, and of myself too. It will not answer to let her whimper about trifles, or to think that I am to be at her feet for ever, but she certainly proves that I am no mean judge of character. She is naturally well-bred, and by no means without sense, a trifle

too devoted. It is an error on the right side,
and I believe she is true as steel. It is a
pity the effervescence of the first days cannot
last. It is heavenly to forget one's self for a
little! I must teach her she is not to have a
finger in any of my special pies, nor to bore
me with her rugged old father. It is rather
a nuisance his being so near a neighbour;
moreover, I fancy he has a shrewd eye for
every change in his daughter's face, and
they are a good many. Only for her
sensitiveness, it would not be so easy to rule
her."

Then he devoted himself to a leading
article he had not had time to "read, mark,
learn, and inwardly digest" in the morning—
an article on the probable composition of the
ministerial majority — over which he fell
asleep, and dreamed he was "asking leave"
to introduce an important Bill to the House
of Commons, and the members were thronging
in from the lobbies, the dining and smoking
rooms, to listen—when the tinkle of a bell
roused him. It was the butler putting the

usual tray with water and glasses on the table.

     *   *   *   *   *

Volumes might be filled with the minute touches which complete the portrayal of a struggle such as was now going on in Janet's heart and mind, its progress, and variations, the brief footholds conquered there, the murderous repulses here, all without visible event, and under the fairest outside.

Yet in that silent battle what cruel wounds were given, what hopes of healing were eagerly grasped, only to slip from the clinging hands, what strength was sapped by the sudden, sultry after-glow of unexpected fits of fondness, which never really melted the rocky substratum of the nature on which they swiftly burnt out. But who would have patience with these dreary details? They must be epitomised. That first parliamentary season in Town, Janet had looked forward to it with such joyous anticipations, and it had been a time of torture. Yet there had been lulls.

Sometimes, when Palliser was pleased with himself, and perceived that he was beginning to be looked upon as a promising member of his party, Janet cheered up, and hope fluttered blue streamers before her eyes. Then they had smart little dinners, with Darrell and Compton and other political men for guests, and the fair young hostess felt more at her ease with her husband's colleagues than with himself. She grew rapidly popular— men did not talk of her beauty, nor quote her clever sayings, but they liked to talk *to* her ; there was a restful tone of sympathetic reality in her conversation—she did not make up her opinions, nor compose her criticisms, she spoke out frankly what she thought, or honestly said she did not know enough to judge.

Lady Darrell came to Town after Easter, of course, and was a tower of strength to her young friend.

Sir Frederic Saville accepted the invitation of a Russian prince, with whom he had fore-gathered at Pau, to join him in a visit to the

Caucasus, and Lady Saville came for a series
of visits to England, the first and longest of
which was to her brother.   Exteriorly, all the
joys and pleasures of life seemed accumulated
round   the   mistress   of   Mervyn   Hall,   yet
few women were more miserable than she
became towards the end of the merry month
of May.

She was always eager to hear Palliser's
speeches, and sometimes surprised him by the
remarks she made on the speeches of others,
but he took care not to tell her of any happy
hit she might have made.

" The season is telling upon you, Janet," said
Lady Saville one evening when she had called
at the House of Commons to take up her
sister-in-law.   "You are looking quite ill—
why don't you go down to Mervyn to recruit?
I never thought you could look so exhausted ! "

" It is not exactly the season—I fancy I
have caught a chill.   It was fearfully hot in
the Ladies' Gallery, then in one of the lower
passages I suddenly encountered quite a cold

draught of air, but I will take a hot cup of tea, and that will do me good."

Mrs. Palliser seemed quite herself that evening at a large dinner-party given by the Marchioness of A——, where there was something of a party gathering, and where she bestowed a good deal of her conversation on that scientific giant, Sir Peter Lyons.

Next morning, however, she had a severe headache, and every symptom of a heavy cold. After a day of mild remedies recommended by Raynes, that excellent woman declared she would not take any further responsibility, and Lady Saville called in the doctor.

The man of healing was a little mysterious.

"Mrs. Palliser had a severe cold. It was impossible to say to what a cold might turn, in another twenty-four hours he could offer a more decided opinion. For the present, Mrs. Palliser must on no account leave her bed."

Next day Dr. Kaye found his patient better, and hoped it would prove an ordinary bad cold, passing off in a few days, but it did not.

There were many fluctuations and a good
deal of fever, her strength seemed to leave
her unaccountably, and as she absolutely
loathed food, the difficulty was to restore it.

Palliser was much concerned, not to say
vexed.   He had arranged two or three
charming little dinners and they had a long
list of evening engagements ; in general, Janet
showed a good deal of tact in the management of her life, but to go and take cold in
the very height of the season was rather unpardonable.   He was, however, anxious about
her and regular in his visits to her room.

Still the doctor said there was nothing
serious about the matter, only Mrs. Palliser's
strength refused to return.   All she cared to
do was to lie quiet.   At last she lost the
power to sleep, and Palliser insisted on calling
in a great doctor, as low fever seemed the
chief malady.   The great man was very kind
and gentle, and asked many questions,
growing graver as he listened.

"She must take nourishment," he said,
impressively.   "She is terribly low ; there is

nothing especially the matter, and yet she seems to have no power to rally. If Mrs. Palliser were not surrounded with all that makes life charming, I should say she did not try or wish to recover. I presume Mr. Palliser could induce her to take nourishment."

" He is always entreating her to try and eat," said Lady Saville, who with her sister-in-law, Lady Darrell, had waited for the doctor in the drawing-room.

"Ah ! doctor, if we could only get a peep into the laboratory of the inner consciousness, what a bouleversement of practice would take place! But no doubt you have methods of introducing sustenance——?" said Lady Darrell.

The great man interrupted her.

" Certainly, certainly, but nothing is so effective as what is willingly taken. The fever, though not very high, is constant and consuming."

" May I see her ? " asked Lady Darrell.

" Of course."

"I'll talk to her a little, and—I suppose she does not wander?"

"No, she says very little, but her mind is perfectly clear. I have written a prescription which may, I hope, secure a night's rest. Meantime, Lady Darrell, you might divert her thoughts for a while—possibly some imaginary annoyance is distressing her."

As soon as the doctor was gone, Lady Darrell ascended to the patient's room. Janet received her with a smile of welcome.

"So good of you to come!" she said, pressing her visitor's hand with her own dry hot one, feebly.

Lady Darrell was greatly shocked at her prostration.

"You know I am not really ill, only so very weak," Janet went on. "I shall come all right, though I don't fancy I shall ever feel young again"—she spoke in a low whisper.

"My dear child," said Lady Darrell, gently but cheerfully, "you will never be right if you do not take food! Forgive me for preaching, but you do not exactly belong to yourself—for your husband's sake you ought to do your best to get well."

"Ah, yes! it would be trying for him if I died. As it is, he must be greatly annoyed!"

"And your father, think how anxious he must be."

"He does not quite know. I have not been able to write for three days, but Gertrude has—she is so kind."

"Would you like to see your father?" asked Lady Darrell, noticing a change in her voice as she mentioned him.

"Ah, yes!" said Janet, with a deep sigh, "it would be a comfort to me to see him, only I do not want to frighten him. My father!" she stopped abruptly, repeated "my father," and burst into a fit of weeping, not loud, but intense, sobbing and trembling from head to foot.

"This is dreadful," said Lady Darrell aside to Raynes, "what shall we do?"

"I believe, my lady, it will relieve her. These are the first tears she has shed, though she used to sigh as if her heart would break,"

and Raynes proceeded to bathe her temples
with eau-de-cologne and water.

Lady Darrell watched her anxiously, and
was presently rewarded by seeing her
gradually grow calmer, then she smiled and
put out her hand murmuring :

" My father ? "

" Yes ! He shall come to you, and we will
be most judicious in the mode of our
invitation."

Soon after this outburst the promised
draught arrived, and when Palliser returned
to dinner, he was met by the joyful intelli-
gence that his wife was sleeping quietly.

He had been in truth desperately anxious
for the last twenty-four hours, and furious
with his sister, the maid, the first doctor,
everyone, once he was aware that his wife's
condition was serious. It seemed incompre-
hensible that she should appear almost
sinking, when there was so little the matter.
He was surrounded with a set of incompetent
blockheads, who were quite capable of letting
a young, healthy creature slip through their

fingers, for want of the commonest care. Why had they not called in Sir James Pennifeather long before?

From the hour that she obtained the relief of tears, the rest of sleep, Janet began to rally. The following afternoon brought Captain Rowley to his daughter's bedside.

So carefully had Lady Saville been in wording her summons, that the stout old sailor received a considerable shock when he first looked at Janet's wasted form; but he controlled himself successfully.

Palliser was more like his old self, unmistakably concerned about his wife, and cordial to his father-in-law.

Captain Rowley was quite happy. Each morning, as soon as the invalid was settled for the day, he went to her room and read the *Times* steadily to her; this performance he considered of the last importance. The great doctor was anxious to get his patient out of bed, and out of town, and as, once she began to mend, she rallied rapidly, in little more than a fortnight, Palliser was discussing the question where it would be best to go for change of air.

"What do you think of Beachurst?" asked Palliser on one of the rare occasions when he dined *tête-à-tête* with his father-in-law.

"It would do right well. The air is more bracing than at most of the South Coast places. Mrs. Bent, Janet's old friend, is settled there too, and would be company for her!"

"It would amuse you too, Captain Rowley," said Palliser, who was in a most amiable mood. "I daresay you would find a good many friends among the naval men there."

"Well, no, I have rather dropped out of it all, still I like to see the blue jackets about, and to smell the salt fresh breeze."

"Yes, of course you do. Try a glass of that port. It is very soft and mellow, all the fire is gone out of it, though there is plenty of body left," and they settled into a serious talk.

When he came to say a few words before

bidding her good-night, Janet observed that her father, though evidently thoughtful, had a very contented, restful expression, and when kissing her before retiring himself, he said:

" Make haste and get well, my dear, if it were only for your husband's sake. He is like a fish out of water without you ! "

And Janet fell into a sweet sleep, lulled by the delicious hope that her possible danger might have brought back her husband's fast fading tenderness, the loss of which had all but dried up the wellsprings of her life.

With the approval of Sir James, the following Saturday was fixed for Janet's journey to Beachurst. As it was a House of Commons holiday, Palliser was able to escort his wife and stay with her till the next afternoon. Captain Rowley was to remain with his daughter, and Lady Saville was to pay her a flying visit occasionally; in the meantime she felt it to be her duty to keep house for her brother, and represent the Palliser interest in society. Janet was perfectly content.

To have her dear dad, and almost daily visits from the Mary Winyard of old days, was bliss. Then Palliser had been so nice and kind at parting. He had kissed her gently and tenderly just as she liked to be kissed, saying :

" I daresay you will look better than ever after this bout of illness—people often rise up quite new creatures from such an ordeal. I hope you'll come back for the end of the season. At all events, I shall come down next Saturday if I can, but I expect I shall have to speak on the following Monday. Of course you get the Parliamentary news here as soon as in town. Don't tire your eyes reading too much, take great care of yourself—good-bye ! "

Janet was greatly cheered by his tone. Perhaps the days to come would be better than those that were past ! but she no longer felt that the light had all gone out of her life when he had left.

Mrs. Palliser and suite were established in the pleasantly-situated " Anchor Hotel," which, as every visitor to Beachurst (and who has not been there?) knows, faces the wide land-locked bay, and the beautiful wooded heights at the opposite side, while to the west, within an easy walk, can be descried the red sand-stone fortifications of Kingsport, above which rise the irregular battlements of the fort. A stretch of green common intervenes between the hotel and the sea, and further inland, a range of low grassy hills sheltered the village and its pretty villas from the north-eastern blasts.

Janet had been little accustomed to the sea, but she loved it, and the weeks she spent at Beachurst were indeed a precious breathing space.

Many a pleasant hour slipped past talking with Mrs. Bent over past days, and girlish adventures, while any letters which came from Maurice were read aloud to his old friend. Janet had heart to interest herself in these things, for hope had woke again and whispered " of bright days to come."

The weather was kind to the convalescent,

25*

and every day she went out to drive with either her friend, or her father.

The latter was quite gay. He had renewed his acquaintance with sundry old shipmates, and used to enjoy his quarter deck walks with them, up and down a wide wooden pier, where in the summer evenings, a band usually played.

Janet had now advanced so much that she used to walk one day, and go out driving another, and looked forward to returning to town and her usual life, in a week or ten days.

"You are as fresh as a four-year old!" said Captain Rowley to his daughter, one bright breezy morning when the air from the sea brought delightful coolness in spite of the glowing sunshine. "I think it would do you good to come out for a stroll with me, and then take your drive in the evening."

"I am sure it would! I will put on my things at once," cried Janet, shutting up her writing book, and a half-written letter to her husband.

"Where shall we go?" she asked, as they

descended the steps of the hotel. " To the
pier ? "

" No ! it is too far for you, my pet ; come
along this way to where the common narrows,
and a corner of the Seacombe woods comes
nearly to the beach. There is a pretty
cottage there, and you can sit down."

The distance was nearly a mile, but a
bench on the wide walk, which ran along a
slightly-raised embankment separating the
common from the beach, gave Janet a rest.

It was a lovely morning, and the delicious
air seemed to pour new life into her veins.
Can it be only material, that glorious consciousness of vitality, that joy in the mere
sense of existence which, when the frame is
young and the spirit unexhausted, at times
swells the heart to such buoyancy, that we
feel as though the thinnest air could make a
pathway for our heaven upheld feet.

Where, as Captain Rowley described, the
woods approached the beach, a pretty little
bungalow, with a wide verandah, was perched
on a knoll, looking westward across the bay,

a small lawn fenced by a wooden paling and studded with much-neglected flower beds, sloped steeply down to the common. The entrance was at the back, and a small bye road led from the main line where the omnibuses plied to and fro, to a suburb which had gathered round some large barracks.

"This might be made a very pretty place," said Janet, looking at it. "I am afraid the house is locked, and I should like to sit down."

"I think there is someone to let us in," said her father. "Can you get so far?"

"Yes, certainly."

The gate was open, and as they crossed the gravel sweep, Janet observed there was a good-sized vegetable garden on the left, and a small conservatory. As they approached, the door was opened from within by a respectable-looking workman.

"I have put a chair in the verandah for the lady," he said.

"Thank you. Come, Janet, my dear, you'll see what a fine view there is."

She followed him with some languid curiosity, and gladly sat down. Captain Rowley,
half leant, half sat on the railing of the
verandah.

"Well, what do you think of the look-
out?"

"It is charming. I could look at it for
ever!"

"That is saying a good deal. Isn't it a
nice drawing-room?"

"Yes; quite a good-sized room."

"Well, there's a dining-room to the front,
not so large, and a little book-room, and upstairs four bedrooms, large and small. What
do you think of that?—and a fowl-yard with
water and a capital pump—never saw a
better."

"Dearest Dad, are you going to take it,
that you are so delighted to show off its good
points?" said Janet laughing.

"Exactly; that's what I'm going to do!"

"Ah," exclaimed Janet, light dawning upon
her, "did Randal suggest this to you?"

"Well, yes, he did. He pointed out that

if at a little distance, I should really see more
of you. You could not run in and out, you
know, which is perhaps as well, but you can
come to me for a fortnight at a time, and I
could come and stay with you, and there will
be lots of old fellows for me to spin yarns
with, and all that, and it is a nice spot to sit
and count the days between your visits, my
pet!" He stopped abruptly, and then resumed. "Your husband has behaved very
handsomely about it, Janet. He is giving
me a fancy price for poor old Navarino Cottage, and—and—I see he has set his heart
on the move, so it is wiser to let him have
his way. It's nearly as cheap as the
cottage, which I don't understand; anyhow,
Palliser's solicitor has settled the whole thing,
and on very good terms. I am getting
a lease of seven, fourteen, or twenty-
one years; that will see the end of me
anyhow."

"Oh, dear, dear father, I don't like it—I
don't like it!" cried Janet, throwing herself
into his arms, and, to his dismay, her tears

began to roll down, though she seemed unconscious of them.

"My pet," said her father, taking out his pockethandkerchief to dry her tears, "you'll do yourself harm, and Janet—listen to me; men are strange, jealous brutes; I saw your husband was set upon my leaving Langford, so I gave in to him. It is better for both of us. He has the whip hand, but he is a man of honour, dear. He'll keep his word, and let you come and see me when you like. You will like it sometimes, will you not, my child?"

"Yes, often — often," murmured Janet, kissing him.

"Remember, Palliser has behaved very handsomely—very handsomely indeed in the matter."

"He is very generous, I know, but oh! so determined to have his own way!"

"Very likely. It's as well not to cross him. Are you rested enough to return?"

"Yes, but I feel quite dazed at the idea of your living here, so far away."

"I might be in the old place, my pet, and yet much further off!"

A week later Janet had returned to her town house, and Captain Rowley had gone back to his pretty old cottage. Everyone said Mrs. Palliser was looking better and more interesting than ever. Her husband distinguished himself in a debate about some small Eastern difficulty, and the season came to a satisfactory ending, in his estimation, at all events.

CHAPTER V.

A CRISIS.

THE fourth season since Palliser's marriage had entered on its second stage, and "all the world" had settled to the struggle of life, social, political, legal, literary, with renewed vigour after the Easter holidays.

Janet had found great refreshment in hers, spent with her father in his comfortable seaside abode, and she returned to take up her part in the drama of London Society, with a slight increase of interest, which she welcomed and cherished as the beginning of a fresh phase of existence.

The few years which have elapsed since last we saw her, were, in point of experience and thorough awakening, equal to a lifetime. She sometimes smiled to herself when she read or heard people speak of "fiery trials" or "heartburnings," and thought that icy repression and slow heart-congealing could be quite torturing enough. During these years her husband had drifted further and further from her, and she had striven desperately to hold him.

First, it was unspeakably bitter to lose his tenderness, then it was almost worse to admit that love in him was represented by a curious mixture composed of taste, gratified vanity, and acquired refinement, dashed with quick, evanescent passion, and that she was striving to hold what did not exist. His relapses into a caressing mood grew fewer and further apart, till, on one occasion when Janet, who was not easily turned from her earnest desire to be conciliating, thinking he looked pale and worn, came close to him, resting her hand on his shoulder, and offered him a kiss, asking, "Are you very tired, Randal?" he put her aside, gently, it is true (he was never rough), but the rebuff was none the less potent. It was the last kiss she ever offered him, and no doubt the growing coldness, of which she was almost unconscious, helped to estrange him.

He had ceased to veil his bitter disappointment at not having a son, especially as the St. Oswald family had been increased by a second. This was a constant source of bitter humiliation to Janet. She felt herself an impostor; she had not fulfilled the end of her existence as Mrs. Palliser, of Mervyn Hall, and this conviction seemed to take from her all sense of right and security, to paralyse her authority, to make her reluctant to lay out her husband's money, or to use her own handsome dress allowance. As her feelings grew refrigerated, and common sense asserted itself, she gathered strength to understand her own position, and force enough to do what was right, whether her righteousness was appreciated or not.

To make her husband's house agreeable to his friends, to give him any help she could in social and political matters, to look as well as she could, these were duties which she carefully performed. The help she could give,

however, was but small.   Palliser had a
secretary, and evidently disdained assistance
from her hands.

Though at first she seemed to recover
quickly from the attack of fever before
described, the improvement was checked
afterwards, and she was for some time in
rather delicate health, a circumstance which
Palliser seemed to resent.   Indeed, she was
never afterwards so brilliant in expression or
complexion, but her face grew more interesting, her eyes more serious, her manner
steadier, her conversation more thoughtful,
while her popularity increased, and she was
rapidly acquiring a certain degree of social
importance among a rather select set, whose
names are never blazoned in the columns of
those curious products of modern journalism,
the weekly gossip papers.

Men liked her heartily, and talked confidentially to her, though they never dreamed
of flirting with her, and her dinners were
becoming recognised as more than ordinarily
well-ordered and agreeable.   She was now

rarely alone with Palliser, and when she was, they were perfectly polite, though she felt that he liked her less and less, and the sense of being alone in the world—save for her father — grew upon her. She was more sympathetic to her brother than she used to be, though his wife somewhat repelled her; but she steadily insisted on inviting them to dinner twice in each season, and left a small packet of Palliser's cards upon Tom in the course of it.

To recommence, Janet was thankful to find she looked forward to the rest of the season, its tasks and duties, with more of interest than she had felt for a long time.

Palliser was to arrive the following day. He had run over to Paris with Darrell, to see Sir Frederic Saville and his sister, who had made that pleasant capital their headquarters, also to pick up some political information, as he, Palliser, was growing more occupied with Parliamentary matters day by day.

Dressmakers, and her visiting list, writing out a plan of dinners and entertainments to fit in with their own invitations, before consulting Palliser on the subject, gave his wife abundant occupation for the first few days of her return.

"Can you give me a few minutes to read over this list of dinners and evenings, and say what alterations you wish?"

Palliser took the paper and pointed out a few changes.

"I wish you would let me see our list of engagements," he added.

"I must have left it upstairs," said Janet, looking into a small velvet bag she carried.

"Never mind, I shall not go out for an hour," he returned; "you will find me in the study."

Having her morning planned out, Janet went at once in search of the missing list, and returned to her husband, who was already writing at his knee-hole table. She laid the paper before him, and standing beside his chair, began to explain how the one list would fit in with the other.

It was very rarely that Janet entered the

study, knowing she was not wanted there. Indeed, from the time they had occupied the house in E—— Square, Palliser's private sitting-room had been more or less forbidden ground to her.

They had nearly finished their discussion, when the butler entered with a note. "Lady waits an answer," he said.

"Lady!" repeated Palliser with a good deal of surprise, "what lady?" and he took the note.

"Well, sir, she looks rather like a foreigner, though she speaks English."

Palliser ran his eye over the lines written within the note. They ran thus:

"Will Mr. Palliser accord the writer a few moments of his valuable time—she has a private communication of some political importance to make?"

The handwriting was strong and masculine, and quite strange to Palliser.

"I suppose I must see her, though I

daresay it is a cock and a bull story," he said, throwing the note on the table before him. " Show her in ! "

" I shall retreat before the political secrets, as soon as she has cleared the doorway," said Janet smiling.

The next moment a tall, stately woman, handsomely dressed in black—not in mourning—crossed the threshold, advanced a step or two, and paused in silence, till she heard the door close behind her. Then she quietly raised and put back her veil, displaying the *beaux restes* of what had been a beautiful face, with fierce dark eyes, and a high colour which was suggestive of high art.

Janet, much struck with her appearance, began to move towards the door, when her steps were arrested by a look of horror in Palliser's face. He rose to his feet, exclaiming as he put out one hand upturned before him—

" Isabel ! my God ! Isabel ! "

" Yes, Isabel ! " she returned with iron steadiness. " Who is *this* woman ? "

Palliser pulled himself together by a great effort, and stepping forward, placed himself between the stranger and his wife.

"Go, Janet!" he said, hoarsely, "leave me. I will come to you presently! Leave me!"

"Are you safe?" she whispered, alarmed at the woman's eyes.

"Go!" was all he could say—and she went.

She was greatly agitated. Palliser's look of horror had stamped itself upon her mind—her imagination.

It was an unmistakable look of fear, and she knew he had fully the average amount of pluck possessed by English gentlemen—fear and horror mingled, as one would feel in the presence of something supernatural.

She sat down in her dressing-room, with an odd, shuddering sensation. She shrank from staying there alone, yet she would not call anyone to stay with her, as she felt that Palliser would soon come, and there must be no witness to their meeting. She felt in some

extraordinary manner, that this terrible
woman must be his former wife, the
unfortunate creature whose charred remains
had been buried some six or seven years
ago !

It was absurd to believe that such a
resurrection *could* take place, yet she knew it
was true. This was Palliser's first wife, and
she herself could be no wife ; but she did not
think of herself, save in brief flashes. What
torture Randal was undergoing ! What an
awful ordeal of exposure lay before him !—all
the old scandal to be raked over again, with
an enormous addition.

How long the woman was keeping him !
How *did* that woman come there ?

Janet was trembling all over—she could
not keep still. She rose and paced the room,
pausing every now and then to look at the
clock on her mantelpiece. A quarter of an
hour, half an hour, an hour, an hour and a
quarter ! She sat down in a corner of the
sofa, and hid her face in the pillow. Would
he never come ?

At last the handle of the door turned and Palliser entered. His ghastly face thrilled her heart with compassion; she had started up at the sound of his approach, and now went forward to him with outstretched hand.

He took and pressed it convulsively, then with a cruel mocking smile, "It seems, Janet," he said in a harsh voice, "that you and I are to be the hero and heroine of a 'penny dreadful' order of tragedy! That infernal woman, do you know who she is?"

"I do," said Janet, growing calm at the sight of his pale fury, "she was your wife."

"Was!" he interrupted passionately. "*Is* my wife, and has come to destroy *you*—to take from you the position to which you are entitled, to bring you and me to shame."

"No, Randal! she cannot do that," said Janet steadily. "How—oh, how is it she is alive, Randal? How can we sufficiently thank God that we have no children?"

Palliser let her go and threw himself on the sofa she had just quitted, exclaiming:

"I am the most unfortunate fellow that ever breathed!" He pressed his hands on his brow. "Yes! that is the only saving point in the whole miserable tangle, and it will enable us to turn her flank!" He stopped—then looking up at her as she stood white, but composed, before him. "It is cruelly hard upon you; another woman would be in hysterics; how fortunate it is that you are not as sensitive as *I* am!"

"How does she come here?" repeated Janet, not heeding this comment.

"That I do not know. I recovered my senses as soon as the first shock of seeing the dead come back to stand before me was over, and felt that I must be cautious in dealing with this devil. Her object of course is to extort money. Had I not recognised her myself, I could never believe any testimony to her being alive. I myself saw her remains! The face was greatly injured, but the hands, the height, the shape (for the figure was much less injured than the face), the hair were hers! We showed a number of photographs to the manager of the hotel, and he picked out hers, as the likeness of the Mrs. Palliser who had come to the hotel the afternoon previous to the fire. There is some infernal story behind all this. My God! to be dragged through the mire again!"

He began to walk the room.

"It is a cruel ordeal," said Janet. "But take courage, Randal, you have been guilty of no wrongdoing, only of imprudence, of youthful folly, and this terrible passage may lead to real freedom."

"It shall," said Palliser, pausing in his troubled walk.

"I did not tell her I was childless. I let her believe she had a firmer grip of me than she has. I asked her how she heard of the birth of my son. She laughed and said, 'Don't you think I read the English papers, whether I am in Europe, Asia, or America, and there I saw the birth of your son and heir at St. Oswald's, where you brought me as an adored bride, where you cruelly discarded me!' You see how the mistake occurred?"

"I do."

"She dwelt with fiendish malice on the disgrace which would hang round both my sons; you see, though she knew I had Mervyn, she never was there, and associated me more with St. Oswald's, where our break-up occurred. I did not undeceive her, I let her imagine that I meditated coming to terms with her. But we parted with the clear understanding that all communications for the future must pass through the hands of my solicitor. I am going to him now, and to-morrow I must speak on the Southshire Branch Railway Bill! It will be difficult to track her course since she vanished, but money and perseverance can do much."

"Then, Randal, I beseech you, try to steady your nerves and do justice to yourself; this is but a temporary trouble, bad as it is; there are long, quiet days at the other side, in which you will have much honourable work to do, and for some weeks at least, little or nothing will be known. You must look across the present storm, and keep your hold on the confidence you are winning from the public."

" I see, Janet, you have not lived with me for nothing. I little thought once that you could ever speak in such a strain. Now I must go to Godfrey. He will think I have lost my senses at first."

" Stay, Randal! " said his wife, flushing up and then growing pale, while she hesitated an instant. " I am sorry to obtrude myself upon you at such a time, but, as in truth I am no longer your wife, what—what ought I to do ? "

" Ah, yes, to be sure. I forgot. I suppose you must not stay here, we must be very guarded, for of course when things are settled, as I trust and believe they will be, and we come together again, it will not do to have continued in the same house together. You had better telegraph to your father, and go to him at once. It is due to ourselves to behave irreproachably in the eyes of the world, and you know, Janet, you can trust *me!* Whatever occurs, my sense of honour will keep me unalterably your husband ! "

" I have no doubt whatever of you, Randal, you *are* an honourable man ! " She paused, for

she could not quite command her voice.
Was this the end of the passionate love which
had sought her so eagerly?—she was to depend
on his sense of *honour*.   But this was no time
to show selfish resentment.   "I shall telegraph at once to my father, but, Randal, I
should like to hear the result of your interview with Godfrey.   When are you likely
to return?   I could take the six o'clock train
to Beachurst."

"It will be a long one, I suspect, but I
shall certainly return before six; you can be
ready to start and I will see you off."

"Of course I may tell my father everything!   Indeed, Randal, it would be better to
make no secret at all of this terrible return
from the grave."

"No, I suppose the sooner it is blazoned
abroad, the better—the sooner the nine days'
wonder will be over.   It will, I fear, be rather a
long affair.   Lest I—lest I should be detained, I
will write you a cheque, for you had better
not lose the six train, and you must not want
any——"

"No—no, Randal," she interrupted, "1 am not your wife, and I will not take your money. I have no debts—I have some of my last quarter and the whole of this one. I have quantities of clothes, and I shall want but little—do not trouble about that."

"I shall communicate with your father on this subject. I shall telegraph if anything occurs to keep me."

He kissed her brow, and left her.

For a few minutes everything seemed a dull blank to Janet, an unreal dream.

The first idea that rose up clear out of the chaotic mist in which she seemed to be enfolded, was her husband's extraordinary indifference towards her.

That in such a crucial moment, no ghost of his former affection revived, showed that it must be dead indeed!

She had evidently then no real home—no real husband to leave. She was going to take shelter with the only heart that was all her own! This was enough for the present. The future?—that must shape itself.

With a curious composure that seemed to her like the outer husk of her mind quite apart from the painful confusion which reigned within, Janet rang for her maid, and gave directions for the packing of her clothes, as she was going to Captain Rowley's for a visit of some duration.

"I shall tell you more when we are there," she added very gravely.

"Thank you, ma'am," said Raynes, with an unmoved countenance, and immediately set about her packing.

What a strange day it was! The endless callers were sent from the door. Mrs. Palliser was not at home to anyone; fortunately she had no special day, and not even Lady Darrell was admitted.

Meantime, Janet was desperately busy. She was rapidly putting up all her letters, papers and memoranda, the few photographs she valued, all the gifts made her by her husband up to the end of the first year of their married life, and other trifling presents from some of his relatives. These packed, she ordered her well-filled jewel case to be placed in his dressing-room.

Time went at once slowly yet swiftly—she strove in vain to eat. It was half-past five when Palliser returned. There was but little time to spare.

"I will tell you as we drive along," he said, and they entered the brougham which was waiting.

Raynes with the luggage had already gone on.

"It will be a tremendous business," said Palliser, as they drove rapidly to Waterloo Station. "At first old Godfrey would not believe me. He insisted that it was a case of mistaken identity. I could hardly persuade him that I recognised her at once. However, he has already put detectives on her track. The difficulty will be to trace her from the time she left London, where she had resided for some time, and disappeared at South-ampton. We are not sure that she is staying at the address she gave. That can be ascertained at once."

"It seems so extraordinary that after disappearing for so long a time, she should hunt you up."

"It is all a matter of £ s. d." returned Palliser. "It will cost a large sum, but none of it shall go into her pocket. I will keep you informed of all that takes place, but I am more hopeful since I have seen Godfrey. I trust, my dear Janet, that you do not think I am to blame in any way? Believe me, I was as certain that woman was dead——"

"You need not assure me, Randal. I am quite convinced that you are blameless—a victim, not a sinner," interrupted his wife kindly.

"To-morrow I shall write to your father. He will probably be the right channel of communication."

A few more words brought them to the station, where they found Raynes and Palliser's valet, who had taken the tickets and secured places.

"Let me know how you get down," said

Palliser, stepping into the carriage after her, "and, Janet, I think it right to say you have behaved remarkably well."

"Have I? There is no time to say more now! Good-bye, Randal, good-bye!" There was a quiver in her voice which touched him.

"I trust all will come right sooner than we expect. Good-bye, dear."

He kissed her kindly and descended to the platform, handing Raynes in with his accustomed good breeding. The whistle sounded, he raised his hat, and in another minute the station was left behind.

It was a clear, balmy, transparent night when Janet and her faithful attendant reached the busy railway station of Kingsport, where they found Captain Rowley awaiting them.

The moment Janet looked at the kind, rugged old face, she saw that her father was racked with anxiety.

"Dearest Dad," she whispered, as she walked down the platform, holding his arm close to her side. "I am quite well, and though I have a curious—a wonderful story to tell you, it is nothing to be uneasy about."

"Your husband?" said the Captain, in a tone full of apprehension. "Where is he?"

"At present he is probably driving down to the House. He came with me to the station, and will write to you to-morrow."

"Then you parted friends?"

"Excellent friends, rest assured of that! And now, dear father, I shall not say another word on any serious subject till the broad daylight."

Janet's tone set the old man's heart at rest, and this being the case, his spirits rose to concert pitch, the usual result of having his daughter with him.

Janet was greatly exhausted after the various violent emotions of the day, and as soon as she had tried to eat some supper and talked a little of the last Parliamentary gossip, she begged leave to retire to her room.

Weary though she was, she lay long awake. It was a warm night, and she left her window open. The soft silence was inexpressibly sweet after the ceaseless roar of London, and the murmuring ripple of waves seemed to woo her lovingly to rest. She reviewed her position over and over again. It was a cruel one!

For more than four years she had lived as the wife of a man, whose real wife was living, and now she had no shadow of claim upon him, nor he on her! In a few days, all London would be telling various versions of the Palliser romance. The Society papers would hint at the probability of extraordinary scandals cropping up in the course of the impending trial. The wits and " diners-out " would make *bon mots* upon the strange affair, and the " Latest Particulars " would be perpetually appearing in the *Southshire Courant* and the *Langford Mercury*. It was a distressing situation for a woman not yet twenty-five. She had mixed in Society under a false name. She ought to be bowed down with shame and humiliation, yet somehow, she did not feel like it! She was

blameless, and it could not touch her. She
had come back to her dear father, and the
sorrow and mortification, the degradation,
the failure, the collapse of her married life
seemed to have fallen from her. Why should
she be afraid of social chatter? She had
married Randal Palliser before God and man,
she had lived openly, and approved by all, as
his wife, and even if the results of the
present extraordinary revolution prevented
her return to him, there was nothing in her
life for which she need blush, nothing to
cut her off from the companionship of the
respectable—only, *if* matters so turned out
that she could not return to her place beside
her husband, her lot would be to dwell in
the shadow of a great misfortune always, and
none could foretell what the eventualities of
the law would be. How was Randal to find
evidence against this dreadful woman? Poor
Randal! she was genuinely sorry for him.
He was indeed the sport of fate¡! , Proud and
sensitive as he was, a more cruel ¡blow could
not have been dealt him.

Then, naturally, the indifference he had shown for herself recurred to her. How steadily it had grown! With what agony she had striven against it, and refused to believe it, now she had no doubt—nor had she for a considerable time past! At present, she was, in a degree, accustomed to the loss of his love, and was growing used to the fading away of her own; she would almost rather have the racking pain of watching, hoping, despairing, back again, than the numb coldness which stilled her soul now. Oh, for the glorious days of light, and warmth, and colour, when his footstep, the sound of his voice, a sudden encounter in the grounds, could quicken her heart-beats and send a delicious thrill through her veins.

What a revelation it had been to talk to him, for Palliser, in certain directions, was a capable and a cultivated man. It was in these more serious conversations that she first perceived a change. He began to find it a trouble to be in earnest with her. Well, it was all gone, all past by, no one would

27*

ever love her as Palliser had done for a short time, nor could *she* believe that any other man would love more constantly. That page of life, therefore, was irrevocably turned over. Her husband had finished with love as far as she was concerned, even the dry bones of the passion had been resolved into their elements—there was nothing to call back to life. Still, she was very, very sorry for him, and hoped he might suffer as little as possible. For herself, the sky looked grey, but a wide horizon lay before her; life is inexhaustible; her brain grew weary, and the murmuring wavelets outside whispered softly of rest and freedom, till, to their caressing music, she fell asleep.

CHAPTER VI.

IT was no light task to tell Captain Rowley her extraordinary tale, but Janet did it fully and vividly.

The old man was greatly upset. At his age difficulties first present themselves. He at once perceived that, however strong the probability of Palliser's resuscitated wife having absconded with some old or new lover, probability without proof was nothing, and Palliser's lawyers were absolutely without any clue to her movements or her history. The uncertainties of the law are proverbial, and it was doubtful how far her desertion would break her marriage. At all events, it was not quite two years after her supposed death that Palliser had married Janet, so,

however matters turned out, that marriage
was void.

"Nevertheless, my dear child, you must
keep up your heart. Things will come right.
This separation will show Palliser the value
of the wife he has been obliged to give up
for a bit!"

The words struck Janet. Then her father
had perceived more than she thought! How
wise and kind his silence had been!

"There's one thing that used to grieve me,
for which I now offer heartfelt thanks to the
good God—you have no children to be dis-
placed from their birthright," he remarked,
after a pause.

"Thank God, indeed!" said Janet in a low
tone, "and thank God I have *you* to come to,
dearest father! Let us be as happy as we
can while we are together. I shall be your
housekeeper; of course, I shall see no one
until this storm be overpast, except Mary—
she will be a great comfort to us both. Will
you, dear, see her to-day, and ask her
to come to me? Tell her all. I do not

feel I could go through the terrible story again."

When Captain Rowley had gone, Janet nerved herself to speak to Raynes, giving her an outline of the truth, and telling her she must return to Town, as she (Janet) had no need now for a lady's maid.

The sedate woman surprised her mistress by the amount of feeling she displayed.

"That such a trouble should come on a lady like you, ma'am!" she exclaimed. "Ah! Mr. Palliser will know what he has lost now!—that he will—and I have seen ladies that did not care half a farthing for their husbands, petted, and spoiled, and made much of, to no end! — and other ways, men a-trampling the sweetest wives under their feet! Of all the contrary things in this life, it is marriage—it always turns up the wrong side!"

"Do not speak so, Raynes! I hope Mr. Palliser and myself do not belong to either class you describe. I trust all will come right. In the meantime, Mr. Palliser will be

happy, I know, to recommend you, so will
Lady Darrell, to whom I shall write."

"Thank you, ma'am, but indeed I should
be happy to stay at whatever salary you
choose, and glad to help in any way. I am
sure the Captain is a gentleman one might
serve with pleasure!"

"I am grateful [to you, Raynes, for your
kindness," said Janet, with moist eyes, "but
it cannot be."

"Anyway, ma'am, I'll go to Eaton Square,
and pack every rag belonging to you—there's
a heap left behind—and if I want more boxes,
I'll just tell Mr. Palliser."

"Very well, Raynes—you know he is only
too ready to give me everything."

"I don't say, ma'am, but he's a generous
gentleman, and if there was law or justice in
the land, they would hang that adventuring
impostor of a woman, and them as has aided
and abetted her, *if*"—she added darkly—
"such there be!"

"Then, Raynes, you must accept——"

"*Certingly* not, ma'am!" with strong

emphasis. "I am Mr. Palliser's employée, and I look to him for my wages."

"Yes, I know, Raynes," said Janet, smiling faintly. "I do not want to take poor Mr. Palliser's debts on myself. I wish to offer you this brooch as a friendly gift," handing her one of wrought gold.

"I am sure, ma'am, your goodness is and always has been great to me." Raynes' voice broke. "I hope and trust soon to see you at the head of Mervyn Hall again—your rightful place—in spite of the schemes and wickedness of them as are trying to put you out. Please to remember, ma'am, I will leave any place to come back to you."

The warm sympathy of Mrs. Bent can be understood. To her (having always pictured Palliser as the most lover-like of husbands) this reappearance of his first wife seemed a trial too hard to bear—her amazement at Janet's fortitude and composure was immense.

"I did not dream you were so strong, dear!" she exclaimed, after a little conversation with her early playfellow; "I do not know how you can endure such a blow."

"My father used to say, ' Needs must when the devil drives,' which is a rough rendering of the impossibility of resisting the inevitable," said Janet quietly.

"Poor Mr. Palliser!" continued Mrs. Bent, "I am awfully sorry for him too!—but life will be all the more delightful when every barrier between you is cleared away."

"The present is a very trying time," and Mrs. Bent fancied the sentence ended with a deep sigh, though she did not understand her friend's dry eyes.

This was the first of many visits; indeed, the intercourse between Janet and her old friend was close and constant. Mary was now the head of a family party—as a sturdy boy of two, and a tiny girl of five months entitled her to a nursery—and it was a real pleasure to Janet to work for them and play with the little ones.

In due course Palliser's letter reached his father-in-law, and was all it ought to be.

Captain Rowley at once handed it to his danghter.

From it they gathered that after an interview with Palliser's solicitors, wherein she learned that her position was considerably weakened by the non-existence of a son and heir, the resuscitated woman had disappeared from the lodging where she had given her address, with the evident intention of giving as much trouble as possible ; but Palliser's agents had already placed her under surveillance, and they had no doubt she would be discovered. Their first effort would be to find her former maid—a very respectable young woman who had left her service only a day or two before her mistress undertook the journey on which she was believed to have lost her life. This maid had since married, and no one knew her present name.

Palliser then proceeded to speak of business.

He proposed an arrangement by which, pending the legal proceedings about to be commenced, a certain income or allowance

should be paid out of the Mervyn estate to
Janet.

"A very proper feeling on Palliser's part,"
said Captain Rowley (they were perusing the
letter together).

"It is a provision I can never accept,"
said Janet in a low, firm voice.

"My dear, I should not say a word on the
subject if I could give you a home such as
you have left."

"Dearest father, do you think I have fallen
so far below my original self that fewer
servants, less elaborately-served dinners, the
necessity for doing a little more for myself,
could make the smallest difference, if—if—
you do not mind taking the burden of my
maintenance on yourself! I shall make but
a small addition for the next year at all
events—and——"

"Nonsense, my pet, I am but too happy
to have you!"

"Thank you, oh, thank you," catching his
hand and pressing it tightly between her own.
"I have to be grateful to you for everything

all my life, but especially for saving me from
the humiliation of taking *his* money."

Her lip quivered, and her voice broke.

"I do not like to hear you speak like this,
Janet," said her father gravely.

"Then you shall *not* hear it again," she
returned, recovering herself. "Believe me, I
will never fail in my duty to my husband."

"I do believe it, but do not fail in love
either—love works wonders."

"I trust you will approve of all I do—but
you will write to Randal, and say we will not
have his money?"

"Very well—but——"

"Oh, I do not want you to write unkindly,
dear. I should like to write myself if I may,
and I will show you the letter. I feel a little
puzzled what I may or may not do under my
very peculiar circumstances."

"The chief thing I fancy is not to meet
more than you can help—just to keep Mrs.
Grundy quiet, you know; but as to writing,
write by all means, it will be a comfort to
him, poor fellow!"

"Perhaps so," said Janet, with a fixed, far away look in her eyes, a sad, soft expression stealing over her face. "Perhaps so!—another difficulty, dear father, has tormented me lately—what am I to call myself? I have no right to the name of Palliser, and anything else seems dreadful, such a badge of—disgrace. It may appear to you but a small matter, yet I am greatly troubled about it."

"No, I don't think it such a trifle!—you must revert to your old name, but you need not hear it very often."

Silence fell upon them a minute or two—then Captain Rowley rose and said;

"I shall write to Palliser at once," and retired to his own little den.

Letter-writing was a somewhat slow process to the old sailor, and before he had completed his task, Janet came and laid her brief epistle beside him.

"I have just read your letter to my father, dear Randal, and thank you for your kind thought of my necessities——you are always ready to give! Do not think me ungracious in refusing your offer, but during this period of separation and uncertainty, I cannot accept money from you. I am sure you will understand my feeling on the subject.

"As for some considerable time I shall live in the strictest seclusion, I shall want very little and put my father to very small expense. Let this question drop then!—you will keep me or my father informed of all that goes on, and try to look forward with hope—for this can be but an episode in your life, though a most painful one. With warmest sympathy in your present trouble,

"I am always yours sorrowfully,

"JANET."

She felt she had no other name to add.

Captain Rowley read it through, and then reperused it without making any remark.

"Don't you like it, dear?" she asked.

"Oh, yes—it's all very nice, but it's not a very wifely letter."

" And I am no wife ! "

" That's true ! I don't exactly understand how the land lies — but don't you be too independent—think of the future."

" I am always thinking of the future," said Janet with a heavy sigh, " and it is even worse than looking back."

Captain Rowley gazed at her with a pained, puzzled expression, and then took up the letter without another word.   Janet bent down and kissed his brow as she left the room.

*   *   *   *   *

It is marvellous how soon the stream of life makes to itself new channels when falling rocks or shifting sands choke up the old ones, and Janet soon settled into the routine of her retired existence, unvaried as it was by any exterior event except Palliser's letters.

By this time a hundred and one rumours had been put in circulation, and curiosity was on tiptoe respecting Captain Rowley's daughter, so that Janet could not bear to walk in any frequented part, so conscious was she of covert looks and backward glances.

There were some woodland walks beyond the Bungalow, where, with her father, she could take exercise, also in the soft summer evenings, they could stroll along the beach beyond the embankment, where only an occasional couple of lovers crossed their path.

It gave her a curious unpleasant sense of imprisonment and espionage, this shunning of her fellow creatures, yet the days were not altogether dreary.

She was at home, really and truly at home, the supreme head of all things. She enjoyed regulating, and even dusting with her own hands. Then she had ample time for reading and music, and never before had she so much letter writing; every creature who had the least right to address her sent sympathising epistles, especially Lady Saville, who promised to pay her a visit as soon as she came to England.

Early in this time of seclusion, she was startled by a most unexpected visitor.

It was a very sunny afternoon, and Janet was writing in the drawing-room, which was kept cool and dark by the outside blinds of the verandah, when the respectable woman, who, with a little girl, did the Captain's household service, entered with a card.

" Will you see the lady, 'm ? "

Janet with surprise and pleasure read " Lady Darrell." She immediately went into the hall to receive her, and found her sitting in one of the " Anchor Hotel " flys, waiting for admittance.

" This is kind and good of you ! " cried Janet. " Do come in. I believe you have come down here on purpose to see me ? "

" I have indeed, my dear ! " resting her hand on Janet's arm as she alighted, and then on reaching the hall, pausing to kiss her gravely. " You are looking, on the whole, better than I expected, though you are thin and worn, and—not the Mrs. Palliser I saw last season ! "

" Come in, dear Lady Darrell ! I am so glad, oh ! so glad to see you." Her voice showed how close the tears were to her eyes.

"You have a charming cottage here," said Lady Darrell, as she entered the drawing-room, which was sweet with flowers and musical with the gentle dash of the waves beyond.

"Come out on the verandah, Lady Darrell, there is a nice comfortable chair, and you can see across the bay from the end."

"Well, my dear child!" said Lady Darrell when she had settled herself, and Janet had drawn a low basket chair beside her. "What an awful business this has been?"

"It has indeed!" said Janet emphatically in a low tone.

"It will make you all the rage, my dear, next season, when everything has been put right. How are matters going on? That dreadful woman has disappeared, I believe?"

"I think they can put their hands on her when necessary. The difficulty is to prove what she has been about since the hotel was

28*

burned; but I have not heard anything for some days. Lord Darrell was kind enough to write to me."

"Yes! he wanted to come here with me, but I told him it would not do."

"Quite right, dear Lady Darrell! I do not wish to see anyone except yourself, or Lady Saville. Now, you must stop to dinner. My father will be so pleased, and we have so much to say!"

"Thank you! I shall be charmed to dine with Captain Rowley and yourself. I am really en route to Brittany, and shall go on to-morrow to Weymouth," and her lady-ship then plunged into a disquisition on the state of affairs. "Nothing has made such a sensation for ages," she exclaimed. "You know people had hardly forgotten about the Palliser separation case, when the Palliser divorce will rivet their attention! Your husband—(oh! yes! everyone looks upon him as your husband)—he is looking awfully ill, everyone feels for him, and for *you*, to be parted in this way, just when you might be a comfort to each other, for you were considered a pattern couple."

Janet smiled sadly.

"You have a charming look-out here," continued Lady Darrell, "and such a pretty miniature house. But it must be very quiet."

"Of course it is, Lady Darrell."

"Suppose you come over with me for a month or six weeks? It would be a complete change and do you good, besides giving *me* pleasure!"

"Many thanks! you have always been most kind to me, but I should be a sorry sort of guest! No, dear Lady Darrell, I shall not quit my father's roof while this dreadful business is hanging over me. This is my proper place, and I do not think my poor father would be happy if I were out of his sight."

"Very likely! I shall leave you my address across the water, however, and if you should fancy a little change, do not hesitate to tell me so, and come over to us."

"I am really grateful to you," said Janet

softly, " but I must stay where I am! I must leave you for a moment to see if my father is in the house."

Lady Darrell looked keenly round while she was away. That is, at the photographs and ornaments, a few water colour seascapes, and a large photograph of Janet in her court dress.

" Hum," said her ladyship to herself, pausing before a small portrait in oils of a naval officer. " The father, I suppose—fine, bluff, sailor-like fellow—would have ' shivered his timbers,' and ' mastheaded ' his youngsters forty years ago, in approved ' Marryat ' style ; there's no one left now to use such cabalistic language. But I don't see Palliser anywhere! He ought to be on her writing-table en-wreathed in forget-me-nots! Here's the writing-table, but no Palliser. She is a brave woman and is bearing up wonderfully, but it doesn't strike me she's breaking her heart about——no, not her husband! It is really extremely awkward. Ah!" aloud as Janet returned, " I am examining all your pretty things, Mrs. Palliser. You have some pretty water colours here."

"They are the work of an old shipmate of my father's, long ago."

"Very nice, I am sure! Who is this neat-looking young woman, who seems to be holding a foaming waterfall in her arms?"

"That is a great friend and former play-fellow, Mrs. Bent. She is the daughter of our Vicar at Langford. She is, as you see, a little overpowered by her baby's robe."

"The man in the surplice is her father, I presume? But who is the young man in the cricketing suit, a bright, honest-looking young fellow?"

"That is Maurice Winyard, the Vicar's eldest son. My father is out just now, Lady Darrell, but he is sure to come in for tea. He will be very pleased to see you, and grateful to you for coming to see me."

"My dear, everyone will be glad to see you. We shall all be giving entertainments in honour of your second nuptials next spring."

"Don't." ·(The word escaped Janet's lips in a tone of entreaty). Lady Darrell continued. "Society will be immensely excited, and grateful to you and Mr. Palliser for the new sensation you are about to bestow upon it. It is really a very curious 'situation' for you. If anything could revive the romance of early married days it would be the sudden appearance of a barrier between you like this. I suppose Mr. Palliser must not come and see you? I believe people in your extraordinary position are obliged to be very careful? I do not offend, dear, in speaking so frankly? It is such a mere unpleasant passing episode, that I consider you still Mrs. Palliser."

"You do not offend or disturb me in the least, Lady Darrell. No one has anything to be ashamed of in the matter, except the wretched woman who deceived Mr. Palliser."

"Exactly so. I knew you would be perfectly sensible and rational about the business," exclaimed Lady Darrell. "You are a very clear, cool-headed young person and

your complete success in London is quite
assured. Already you are a most interesting
topic of conversation."

"Which is small matter to me," returned
Janet with a sigh.

"My dear, you are not going to sentimen-
talise on the top of my panegyric on your
sound——"

"No, Lady Darrell, but," smiling, "I feel
dreadfully tired sometimes—of everything."

"Ah, that is nervous depression; the result
of the shock you have had. I wish you
would go abroad with me. The change
would do you a world of good. I will talk
to your father about it."

"Pray, do not, Lady Darrell! It would be
useless. I shall not quit my father's roof
until——"

She paused.

"Yes," put in Lady Darrell, "I know;
until you return to your husband's. Perhaps
you are right. By the way, my son desired
his best remembrances to you. He sorely
wanted to pay you a visit, but I absolutely

forbade him. You must see no men, my
dear, except your father, your brother, and
perhaps the husband of a friend *in* his wife's
presence."

Here Captain Rowley walked into the room
and stopped short, greatly surprised to find
his daughter engaged with a very distin-
guished-looking stranger.

A word of introduction, however, explained
everything, and the kind old man's face
brightened at this token of regard to his
beloved daughter.

The afternoon was really a pleasant one
to the shrewd dowager, who was extremely
active and took a lively interest in the affairs
of her few favourites. She looked through
the house, examined Captain Rowley's small
collection of curios, coins, and oddities,
gathered in many lands, and even visited the
little fowl yard, where she put the cook
through an examination, and recommended a
special mixture of food.

Then she took a walk with Janet, after
which she quite enjoyed her dinner, and pro-

nounced everything excellent with a certain heartiness absolutely free from condescension.

"By George!" exclaimed Captain Rowley, when he had put his guest into the fly brought for her at ten o'clock by the confidential man-servant who always travelled with her. "That is a sort you don't meet every day; a great lady, if you will, but a sharp business woman into the bargain. Why, she was as keen about that idea of getting a bit of the rough ground outside the garden cheap and starting a poultry farm, to supply the ships, as if she had earned her bread all her life. But you are looking pale and fagged, my pet, eh?"

"Yes, dear, I am very tired. There was no news from Randal to-day."

"No; the poor fellow hadn't time to write, I daresay. Faith, I admire his self-command and respect for you, always sending the letters to me, which answers the same purpose, eh?"

"Yes, it is admirable. Good-night, dearest father."

CHAPTER VII.

LADY DARRELL's visit cheered and comforted Janet.

She was naturally brave, and by no means subject to nerves, fancies, nor depression, but of late she had been less physically strong, and times of weakness come to the strongest.

The drop from constant and brilliant society, distinction, observance, to seclusion and careful avoidance of notice, was a big one, and sometimes jarred upon her, while again, the sense of being supreme, the chief object of love and consideration in her father's simple home, gave it a charm of repose and peace, which she had long ceased to find in her husband's. Meantime Palliser's letters kept her informed of the progress made in preparing for the impending divorce suit, sometimes addressed to her, sometimes to Captain Rowley. Their tone was friendly, but the lover had evaporated.

The future presented a very sombre aspect to Janet; the more she looked at it, the more formidable it seemed, till she shrank from its contemplation, taking refuge in any subject, any employment to escape from thought.

It was a week after Lady Darrell's visit, and she had gone to spend the day with Mrs. Bent and her babies, as Captain Rowley had gone with an old messmate for a cruise round the bay and to a little fishing hamlet, which was beyond the southern headland, on the open sea.

"There is something the matter, Mary," she exclaimed, when they had exchanged greetings. Her friend's eyes looked like tears, and there was something restless in her manner.

"There is, indeed," she returned. Have you seen to-day's paper?"

"No."

"There is an account of poor dear Maurice

in to-day's *Times*," said Mrs. Bent, "only a telegram, though a long one. It seems there has been a totally unexpected outbreak of a hill tribe, whose name I cannot pronounce, somewhere on the eastern frontier, and a small party of English troops was surrounded in the village. The commander managed to telegraph to the nearest station, where they had not many soldiers either. There was a company or two of Maurice's regiment there, and somehow he was sent in command. At all events, they had a terribly difficult night march, and he seems to have managed wonderfully well, and against greatly superior numbers too! He held the insurgents at bay till a larger force came up, but he is severely wounded. These telegrams are dreadful things—it will be quite three weeks before we can possibly have any particulars, meantime we just know the worst. Poor dear mother, she will be terribly anxious! I will get you the paper!" and she hurried away. How diligently they pored over the brief details of the telegraphic despatch. The sister, chiefly concerned about her brother's probable sufferings and loneliness, away from the loving care and companionship of his kith and kin—the friend, almost as excited at the splendid chance thus offered for an upward stride in his career.

"He ought to do well now, Mary!" she exclaimed, "after proving he possesses such soldier-like qualities! It seems to me quite incredible that Maurice, who was so easy-going, so devoted to games and sport, so young of his years—I am sure I feel ever so much older than he is—should command a number of men, and be equal to such a tremendous affair! I feel quite proud of him!"

"You never appreciated him, Janet," said Mrs. Bent, tearfully, "because he was perfectly straight and simple, and thought so little of himself—you overlooked him! *We* all knew how we could depend upon him, and trust him. He always seemed to know what was best to do, even when we were quite children, and you and he used to quarrel; he always took care of us, and knew his way all over the country. He was so gentle too, no one seemed aware how strong and brave he was—he never gave a thought to himself! No, Janet! you never appreciated Maurice, and he was *so* fond of you."

"You have painted a hero, Mary," said Janet, with a far-away look in her eyes. "Perhaps I did not do him justice, I was so vain and selfish then. Oh! how much I have learned since! Now, Mary dear, you must not fancy your brother is going to die; you know how healthy he is, and though not at home, he will have excellent care. You must determine to believe he will recover quickly, until you hear further. When can we have the full account?"

"This is the third—oh! not certainly for three weeks! I must write to poor dear mother, Janet."

"Yes, you must; and may I put in a few lines?"

"Oh yes, do! she will be delighted, she was always so fond of you!"

"And always so good to me! While you write, Mary, I will get the map and look out this place, Chandrapur—it must be a very mountainous district."

From this startling news the friends could not get away. It took them back to early days, to the tears, the joys, the battles, the reconciliations of childhood and budding youth, till their reminiscences reached the epoch of the ever-to-be-remembered ball given by Palliser in celebration of his return to reside in his ancestral hall.

Here Janet paused and contributed no more to the stream of recollections. She kept silence while her friend continued to speak, till her stillness attracted Mrs. Bent's attention. She stopped, and looking somewhat earnestly at Janet, saw that she was white and that her lips quivered.

"My dear," she began, when Janet broke down, and bursting into tears, covered her face with her hands, sobbing for some minutes as if her heart would break.

"Do not, dear!" said Mrs. Bent, with some

vague idea of consoling her. "Of course it
is dreadfully trying now, but after all, it is
only an exercise of patience. A few months
and all will be right again, you will be in
your proper place by your husband's side.
Just think of his joy to welcome you back,
and——"

"Don't!" interrupted Janet, starting up
with an impatient gesture, walking towards
the door and returning, "I am contemptibly
weak! Talking of those sweet old days was
too much for me. You know I never dare
cry at home, for I feel my dear old Dad
watches me keenly, to see if I am fretting or
not. Oh, Mary, of all the blessings God has
given us, the best, the most merciful, is that
we are kept from a knowledge of the future!"

"Still, dear Janet, I think that your future
promises to be very bright, you must keep up
your heart by looking at it."

Janet made no reply, she slightly shook her
head, and pressing her handkerchief to her
eyes, leant back in her chair, and seemed by
her stillness to have gained self-possession.

The appearance of Mrs. Bent's little son with "a nice clean face" and snowy pinafore, ready for dinner with "Mamma" at luncheon time, gave a pleasant turn to the current of their thoughts. Janet was glad to take him on her knee, and explain to him for the twentieth time, the uses and history of the many charms which hung at her watch-chain.

*　　*　　*　　*　　*

So take the readers through the dreary painful details of a divorce case, is but to repeat a species of literature with which they are but too familiar in the daily papers.

A summary of the tracing and piecing together of the curious story finally laid before the Divorce Court, will suffice.

When Isabel Palliser, *née* Felinski, daughter of a Polish father and an English mother, found that her husband was determined to separate from her completely, when the history of her past became known to him, and that the continuance of her comfortable income depended on her conduct, she made

29*

up her mind to prudence and fair-seeming. For a considerable time she kept her resolution well, partly strengthened by the knowledge that she was extracting a solid yearly sum from Palliser's pocket.

In time, however, an irreproachable life grew intolerably wearisome. The sameness, the dull routine, the suppression — above all, the absence of men's society became more than she could endure. She might have held out a little longer, but for two events which, though unconnected, acted in unison on her already shaken constancy.

First, the quiet solemn English lady's maid whom she engaged after she had parted with her husband, had given notice to quit, as she was going to be married. This woman had been looked upon as a guarantee for respectability by her mistress, who stood slightly in awe of her immaculate air, but retained her in her service, as a sort of screen or buffer against the inquisitive researches of Palliser's agents, for she knew she had been closely shadowed for a long time, though the watch was now somewhat relaxed.

Feeling that the present was a chance for change and freedom, she ventured to plan a little excursion abroad with the only one of her former friends, with whom she had kept up any correspondence.

Madame d'Almaine was a lady of large experience and cosmopolitan tastes, American by birth, French by marriage and adoption. No longer young, her tastes and pleasures had subsided from the wilder indulgences of youth to the more sober and lasting joys of—not exactly gluttony, but certainly of avarice ; she had always managed to preserve a certain outward propriety and looked on herself as a person of the highest respectability.

As Mrs. Palliser's misfortunes left her well provided for, her friend always sympathised warmly with her, and even came to pay her a consolatory visit in her pretty little abode at Kensington. While Mrs. Palliser cogitated this expedition, all her plans, intentions, resolutions were shivered and reduced to their original elements, by a sudden encounter with an old lover, of whom she had once been passionately fond, Colonel Desvœux, a handsome well-bred American adventurer, from the Southern states, who was fresh from a swindling campaign in Paris, and flush of cash.

A thirst for the old reckless life of excitement and passion overpowered her ; for a moment she was inclined to throw everything to the winds for his sake, but he reminded her that she would have to live, when the fit was over. They therefore decided not to risk too much, and concocted the following scheme, which would secure them a few delicious weeks in each other's society without running much risk.

Among Desvœux' numerous acquaintances was a certain Mademoiselle Adèle, one of the dubious Parisians who enliven our dull capital. She had a slight—perhaps more than slight— likeness to Isabel, she was of the same height, much the same graceful figure, abundant black hair, and flashing dark eyes ; she spoke English fluently, though with a foreign accent.

This interesting young woman was engaged

to personate her employer's friend, and was to start with her for Southampton, the port chosen partly because Madame d'Almaine was sojourning at Havre, partly because that route was less used by persons likely to recognise the fascinating Colonel. For a consideration Mademoiselle agreed to change clothes and trinkets with her temporary mistress and go to an hotel with that lady's luggage, duly addressed "Mrs. Palliser." Next morning she was to take the steamer to Havre where, also for a consideration, Madame d'Almaine would receive the accommodating demoiselle.

At Southampton Desvœux was to meet his fair friends, and here they would part company with Adèle.

His intention was to make for Bordeaux, and cross the frontier into Spain, and after a month or six weeks with his charming companion, he was to make his way back to Yankeeland, while she was to join her friend Madame d'Almaine in Paris and make her way to London.

All went well. Mrs. Palliser bid her English maid good-bye in the kindest manner and dismissed her with a handsome present, saying another attendant awaited her at Havre.

Then she visited her bank, spoke with her usual politeness to the manager, mentioned her intended excursion and drew a moderate sum for the journey, adding that she would write when she required more; afterwards she saw her doctor, who took a great interest in her and was quite pleased to find she was going to have a change. So far all went well, but——

Adèle retired somewhat early for her, and continued to peruse a thrilling romance after settling herself on her pillows, by the light of a candle carelessly placed on the bed beside her. She had enjoyed a hearty supper, and a bottle of sparkling Moselle, so not even the scorching love and fierce revenge of her novel could keep her awake; the book dropped from her hand and overturned the candle, slowly the sheets and curtains ignited, thick smoke stifled her before the alarm was given—when

at last the door was burst open clouds of
smoke delayed the efforts to succour the
victim, whose blackened, half-consumed face
and throat showed there was no hope of re-
calling her to life.

When Desvœux and his companion heard
of the catastrophe next morning they were
aghast. Whatever was the result, Isabel's
career as Mrs. Palliser was at an end.

Desvœux managed to persuade the people
at the hotel to let him see the remains.
" The face is greatly disfigured," he said when
he returned to his accomplice. " But there's
a lot of hair left. The watch and chain
are preserved, and some of the rings are still
on the right hand. The inquest will be held
this afternoon. A hundred to one she will
be buried as Mrs. Palliser. As to tracing
Adèle, I don't suppose there's a soul to
trouble about her. Her pals in London think
she is gone to America with me, and the
sooner we are off the better. The Hamburg
steamer to New Orleans touches here this
evening, let's sail in her! You can never

account for yourself! I'll stick to you, we make a pile together, or if we fail, clear out together. Let us have a good time while we can. By-and-bye that fool Palliser will marry, then when his son is a couple of years old, he will stand a round sum, or a big annuity to prevent his heir being publicly bastardised," so the Colonel and his companion vanished from the scene.

After some years of a not unhappy life, according to their standard, the Colonel was shot in a street row, out West. Isabel mourned him with sincere sorrow. Then finding her fortunes at rather a low ebb, she started for Europe to blackmail her unfortunate husband.

Such was the extraordinary story painfully put together by the keen and experienced detective employed in this difficult case. It took time, however, to collect the many morsels which formed the curious mosaic, and it was not until the early days of December that Palliser's solicitors were ready to go into court.

The unscrupulous woman who had hoped to deal so terrible a blow, was penniless, and too crushed by her signal failure, to make any attempt at supporting what she saw was a hopeless cause. The case was therefore undefended, and was consequently not "long drawn out." It nevertheless excited great attention. The Society papers had numerous paragraphs on the subject. *The Morning Thrasher* had a long leader, distributing impartial blame all round. *The Conservative Banner* attributed the scandalous circumstances to moral decay, consequent on democratic principles, and every print throughout capital and counties, availed themselves of such material for "copy" during the dull season.

It was an excruciating time for Palliser. The "decree nisi" which closed the hearing, and made him a free man, hardly compensated for all he had endured. He had abundant evidence of his popularity in the sympathy and regard shown him by his friends and acquaintances—but the trial left him exhausted, and he gladly took the advice of his doctor, called in to minister to a severe cold, and set out rather suddenly for a trip to Egypt.

Of this move Janet was apprised by the following letter :

"MY DEAR JANET,

"You will have heard the news last night !—I am almost too dead beat to be glad, besides, it was a foregone conclusion. I trust you have felt less harassed than I have been. As this decree does not come in force for six months, and I am warned to be extremely cautious during that period, I think it wiser to deny myself the pleasure of seeing you before I start for Alexandria, where I propose spending two or three months in the hope of recovering health and spirits. Would you like to go abroad anywhere ?—if so, do not hesitate to draw upon me. I will let you know how I get on in the land of the Pharaohs. Callender of Grangemuir and Barnard, the water colour man, are to be my travelling companions as long as we like

each other, so I shall not be bored. I hope
to return quite myself, when we shall put
all matters right, and I shall make a fresh
Parliamentary start. Pray write to me.
Godfrey will forward your letter, and I will
let you know my future address.

" Yours affectionately,

" RANDAL PALLISER."

CHAPTER VIII.

AN INTERLUDE.

THIS epistle arrived by the first post, and was sent up to his daughter by Captain Rowley—under cover to whom all her letters came, to avoid the awkwardness of addressing her by her former appellation.

"Well, and what was the news from that husband of yours?" asked the old man, when she appeared at breakfast, looking white and worn, but quite composed. "I suppose he doesn't know whether he is on his head or his heels now that he is a free man."

"He is frightfully weary and done up, poor fellow! I will give you the letter after break-fast—my head aches, and I am longing for a cup of tea."

"Why didn't you have your breakfast sent

up to you, my pet ?—you fancy you are made
of iron ! Here, here's a leader on your case
in the *Daily News*, very well written, and
complimentary to Palliser—'pon my soul, I
couldn't have done it better myself ! No—I
don't mean *that* "—in answer to a quiet smile
from Janet —" I mean I couldn't have backed
him up better myself. This horrid business
won't do him the slightest harm ; on the
contrary, you'll both start on higher ground
than ever."

" I earnestly hope Randal will not suffer in
any way," she said gravely, as she applied
herself to her cup of tea.

" I'll have no end of congratulations at the
club to-day," resumed Captain Rowley ; " all
the fellows there have been uncommonly keen
about the case."

" There could be but one conclusion,"
returned Janet, whose extreme quiet con-
trasted with her father's fidgetty excitement.

He did all the talking during the meal,
and was a little vexed that his " pet " put
aside the newspaper he handed her, and

seemed averse to read the "leader" which pleased him so much.

When Janet saw that her father had breakfasted she drew the letter from her pocket, saying :

"There is a nice fire in your 'den,' dear, shall we go in there for a good talk?"

"By all means, and I can have my pipe."

Janet took up her knitting which always lay at hand—and Captain Rowley put on his spectacles, but forgot his pipe in his anxiety to read his son-in-law's letter. There was profound silence until he had finished— then he threw it on a table that stood by his armchair.

"By George!" he exclaimed, and then paused, his face flushing, "I have always tried to be sensible and hold my tongue—but —by George! that's a d——d cold-blooded, selfish letter to write to a woman—a wife— that's gone through such a trial as you have, like an angel—damn me!—like a regular brick."

"You must allow for differences of nature

and temperament," said Janet, with a slight sigh. "I am not disappointed, he does not mean to be unkind; it is quite true we must not be together—we have a most malignant enemy who is ready to avail——"

"But, good Lord!" interrupted her father, "fancy a man going off to recruit his health and take care of himself without coming to see how his wife — and such a wife — has stood the strain of such a time of trouble— and give her a parting kiss. Why, the fellow must have water instead of blood in his veins."

"There's no good discussing the matter, dear dad!— there it is, we can change nothing."

"Well, Janet, I think it is your duty to show more spirit and self-respect than to take this neglect tamely, without remonstrance— I'd—I'd——" he stopped abruptly, annoyed with himself for having said so much.

"You think so?" said Janet, raising her eyes to him with a sudden light in them, "perhaps you are right! Dearest father, I

will think carefully of the future which lies
before me, and speak to you when—when
I have something to suggest — but for the
present, let us be happy together—for no
shadow ever comes between our hearts, and,
oh—to be with you is indeed to be at home
and at rest! Do you remember that next
Thursday is the anniversary of my wedding-
day?" Her voice broke, and sinking at her
father's feet, she leant her head against the
old man's heart, and wept quietly but bitterly
for some minutes. While he consigned himself
to very warm regions for a blethering old idiot
—to have let his tongue loose and suggested
unhappy thoughts to her.

"I am very weak too, dear," she said at
length, mastering her emotion, "but we are
not going to bemoan ourselves any more. I
shall write a kind letter to Randal—*I* know
what torture he has undergone since this
extraordinary resurrection of his first wife!
I shall never forget her—she must have been
a beautiful woman when younger."

"Yes !—he had deuced good taste,"

returned Captain Rowley grimly. "So you'll write to him to-day—well, Janet, as you are going on a smooth tack, don't you think you might hint that it would be more decent to come down here, even for a couple of hours?"

Janet thought for a moment and then said quietly :

"No, I shall make no suggestion."

"As you will, my dear, and about the trip abroad?—it might do you good, and you have every right to use his money."

"No, a thousand times no!" she cried with some heat, "we will have a cosy winter together, you and I, and forget that we were ever parted! I shall go and write my letter, and remember you never say a word against Mr. Palliser, dear dad, nor hint at my taking any of his money! I feel thoroughly unmarried."

"But you'll take it when you are re-married?"

"Oh! when I am remarried, of course I will!" and she left him, turning at the door

30*

to kiss her hand to him, with a sweet frank smile.

The next week was fully occupied answering congratulatory letters, which poured in from everyone who had the slightest right to address her, and sundry of the higher officials of Kingsport Dockyard and their wives left their cards upon her, which put her in a small difficulty, as she did not like to return them with her own, either as Mrs. Palliser, to which name she had no right, or as Mrs. Rowley. She therefore kept indoors, and begged her kind friend Mrs. Bent, who knew most of the society at Beachurst, to make her excuses and explanations.

All through this time of trouble, Mr. and Mrs. Tom Rowley had been most friendly and sympathetic. Indeed, Mrs. Tom was prouder than ever of her grand relations, as she considered the Pallisers, since they were the objects of a " cause célèbre." Just before Christmas she wrote a most pressing invitation to her father-in-law and Janet to pass the festive season with them in their grand brand new house. For Tom had practised and prospered to his heart's content, and Janet was now aunt to two immensely fat, red-headed boys—" regular Rowleys "—their satisfied mother declared.

To this proposition Janet could not bring herself to agree; she strove in vain to persuade her father to accept it, as she thought it might cheer and amuse him, but he was inflexible, and while they were discussing how to decline with sufficient conciliatory politeness, a letter from Lady Saville arrived, informing Janet that she was in London, having been unexpectedly called over from Hyères, where she had been nursing Sir Frederic, whose health had been much broken during the last year.

" I am longing to see you," she went on, " and if you will have me, I will go down to the ' Anchor' for two or three days at Christmas, to have an outpouring of confidences, so reserve all my news till we meet. I hope Randal is well! He hasn't honoured me with

a letter for ages.   Pray give my love to your
dear father.

"Always yours affectionately,

"G. Saville."

"I shall be *so* glad to see her!" cried
Janet. "Though her letters are few and far
between, she never forgets me. Don't you
think, dear Dad, we might take her in
altogether? She might have my room—the
little one at the back would do for me,
then."

"I'd be right glad to put Lady Saville
up!" he interrupted, "but how the deuce
should we manage about her Ladyship's
Lady? There's the rub! She'd turn up
her nose at her quarters till it would never
come down again. We couldn't put her in
the kitchen to dine with that old frump
Mrs. Brown, and the girl, she'd give them
fits! No, no, my pet, let Lady Saville put up
at the Hotel, and dine every day with us."

"Perhaps it would be better," returned
Janet reflectively, and remembering the

difference between Mervyn Hall and the Bungalow.

This promised visit furnished a valid excuse for declining Mrs. Tom's invitation, and cheered Captain Rowley greatly. During the succeeding week he was exceedingly busy with hammer and nails, and the "high steps," putting up fresh curtains, rectifying locks, and fastening list round the doors. Carpentry of all kinds was a joy to him; once indeed, in the winter time, he even made a cabinet. This employment possibly prevented his noticing the profound preoccupation of his daughter. She was constantly in deep thought, and left all the talking to her father. She wrote a good deal, though she did not post many letters.

Randal wrote from time to time, but irregularly, often very briefly; sometimes Janet did not reply, but rarely left more than one unanswered. Captain Rowley was inclined to fidget when she did not write.

It was a wild, stormy evening, two days before Christmas, when Lady Saville arrived.

Captain Rowley went to meet her at the station and conduct her to her hotel, where he waited to escort her to his cottage when she was ready.

Janet was surprised at her own agitation on meeting her—no, she was no longer her sister-in-law—her friend, and pained to find her looking wan and worn.

"This is nice!" exclaimed Lady Saville, embracing her warmly. "You look so delightfully warm and comfortable here, but, dear Janet, you are a shadow of yourself! You are so thin and white! I am sure if Randal saw you he would be, or ought to be, flattered. I am not very flourishing either— nursing does not agree with me, and Sir Frederic is rather a difficult invalid, poor fellow!"

"I am so very, very glad to see you," was all Janet could say, and Lady Saville, seeing that she could not quite command her voice, went on talking:

"Your father is the best and youngest of us all! I was so glad to see him at the station. How good of him to come out in such weather! Ah! my dear Captain Rowley, men of a—let us say—certain age monopolise all the chivalry and politeness that is left in the world—the young men are sunk in selfishness."

"Ah! my lady," as he sometimes termed her jestingly, "you make too much of an old salt. Come, sit down in this easy chair and toast yourself while we are waiting for dinner."

"I am sorry to hear that Sir Frederic has been so ill," said Janet, who had quite recovered herself.

"He took a severe cold last spring which turned to bronchitis; he was better in the summer, but he had another attack this autumn, and now he is tormented with gout as well—can you imagine it?—he does not like me to leave him for a day, and I have grown *so* amiable—I have immense patience really! But, oh! it is a relief to get away for a little rest. I shall return to my post in about ten days, and do my best for him, poor man!"

Here dinner was announced, and as Lady Saville took her host's arm she exclaimed :

" There, let us not mention anything painful for the rest of the evening. I want to be happy for a while, and make you both brighten up. You have no business, Janet, to look so white and doleful, with all the excitement of a fresh wedding before you."

" Do not speak of it ! " exclaimed Janet, with a sudden irresistible shrinking which Lady Saville did not seem to notice.

" You will be enormously the fashion, my dear Janet, I assure you," she went on, as she took her seat. " Society will be quite obliged to you and Randal for a new sensation, will it not, Captain Rowley ? "

" There is no accounting for the whims of Society," he returned, with a quick, uneasy glance at his daughter. " Tell me what news have you of your soldier son ? "

" My dear Alec ? Very good, I am happy to say. He likes India very much ; I am afraid he is in rather an expensive regiment, but it can't be helped ! He had a very sharp attack of fever some months ago, and I cannot tell you how good and kind Captain Winyard, your old friend, was to him—his sister lives here, doesn't she? I must go and see her and tell her to thank her brother for me."

"She will be delighted to talk about Maurice. Where is Alec's regiment quartered?" asked Janet.

"At Rawul Pindi, but they are to be moved soon, which I regret; I think Captain Winyard is an excellent friend for my boy. He is in a native corps, but has been acting aide de camp to Sir Charles Hepburn for some time—I fancy he will get on very well."

The conversation flowed away from Janet and her affairs to her immense relief. She enjoyed Lady Saville's bright, sympathetic talk. After dinner, Captain Rowley discreetly remained in the dining-room to enjoy his habitual "forty winks," and Janet held some graver converse with her sister-in-law, who confided to her something of her trials as sick nurse to her husband.

"He is terribly trying," she said, "but I am infinitely sorry for him. Now that he cannot ride, or hunt, or go to jovial dinners with amusing, disreputable people, he seems to have nothing left—not an interest in the world! I suppose I should not be much better myself in my way. It is really awful! Then he cannot bear me out of his sight—he wants me to do everything for him, though really his man is a capital nurse."

"At least, it is gratifying to find you are so necessary to him!"

"I cannot say it is," returned Lady Saville, with a little, low laugh. "You must not suppose that he is lovingly dependent on me! He is as cross as a hundred cats, and finds fault with everything I do, poor fellow! I am so glad to be with you for a while, and yet I shall be uneasy till I return to him. Oh, Janet, he was so handsome, and gay, and charming, I look at him in amazement sometimes. I really think he dislikes me now and then. Isn't it curious? Then he doesn't care a straw for the boys—by the way, Fred

is doing very well at Cambridge. He has
more brains than Alec, but he is less loveable.
Darrell has been very nice to him, and makes
him an allowance—that reminds me, I saw
Darrell yesterday. He said he was coming
down here to see you and Captain Rowley.
He is going to Devonshire, I think. Darrell is
growing quite steady. He had rather a wild
youth, I fancy."

Lady Saville did most of the talking until
Captain Rowley joined them. Then she
suggested whist with dummy, which greatly
pleased her host. He loved the game,
though he was by no means an expert, and it
seemed to him ridiculously early when the
carriage for Lady Saville was announced.

When Lady Saville arrived next day,
Janet was surprised and pleased to find that
Lord Darrell accompanied her.

She received him cordially enough. Yet a
strange sense of shy awkwardness made the
colour rise in her pale cheeks. How vividly
his presence recalled Mervyn in those first
heavenly days of supreme content. He had

always been a good friend, and had shown
more of his heart and mind to her than any
one else, save perhaps his mother, had ever
seen.   He was shrewd and sensible, with
touches of finer feeling than people suspected.
He looked bigger, redder, more bony than
ever, but Janet noticed that he gazed gravely
and searchingly at her, as if he wished to see
how she had stood the strain of the last eight
or nine months—she observed, too, that he
called her Mrs. Palliser as in former times.

"I took the liberty of coming down here
uninvited," he said, after they had exchanged
greetings, "as I thought you would like to
hear the latest news of Palliser.   I have come
straight from Cairo."

"Indeed," cried Lady Saville, "you did
not tell me."

"Well, I only saw you for five minutes,
and you had a good deal to tell *me !* "

"Which means that I talked so much you
could not put in a word."

"Do not invent such a speech for me.
However, I have been up the Nile.   I met

Palliser when he first came out — he was rather a wreck, poor fellow; then I saw him afterwards at Philae, and he was quite himself—quite keen about an excursion into the desert after he had reached the second cataract. He talks of returning about the end of February. Barnard has been doing some splendid work, he gets the atmospheric effect of blazing heat wonderfully. Palliser seems enjoying the trip immensely."

" I am very glad to hear it," said Janet earnestly. She had listened eagerly to Darrell's report. " And you think he is quite well and strong ? "

" I should say better than he has been for a long time. He will come up blooming for the happy re-union that awaits you both. Why, Mrs. Palliser, you and your husband beat the record of all the sensational novelists by a long way. What an extraordinary story."

" It is, indeed," cried Lady Saville. " It was almost the only thing poor Sir Frederic cared to talk about. He wanted to know the

minutest particulars, but I don't think Janet
cares to talk about it, she looks so ghastly
white. It has been a dreadful time! It is
so bright and fine to-day, and not at all cold,
suppose we take a nice, long walk. I have
grown quite fond of walking since I have
leave of absence every day for an hour's
exercise."

These few days passed very pleasantly.
The quartette were constantly together—
Captain Rowley enjoyed taking Darrell over
some of the ships, new and old, the latter
being a keen yachtsman, and, the old sailor
admitted, wonderfully wide awake for an
amateur.

Lady Saville paid more than one visit to
Mrs. Bent, who was greatly gratified by her
praises of Maurice, and her husband—like
most men—was quite charmed with the
gracious little lady. They had much talk
about Langford and its people. Mr. and
Mrs. Bent were going to spend New Year's
Day and the rest of the week with her
mother, who, of course, adored her grand-

children, and Janet begged Lady Saville not to desert her and her father, till that festival was over.

To this she assented, while Lord Darrell offered to stay and escort his aunt as far as Paris on her homeward journey.

It was a pleasant interval to Janet. She felt the charm of congenial society; she was grateful for the welcome attention, but her heart and spirit were depressed by the weight of an important decision over which she had thought long and deeply. She did her best to be a sympathetic companion, and succeeded fairly well. And when, on the third day of the new year, Lady Saville and suite departed for " London *en route* for the Continent," as the Kingsport *Weekly Intelligencer* informed its readers, Janet could not quite restrain her tears.

" I hope to Heaven," said Lady Saville to her nephew, as they settled themselves in their carriage, " I hope to Heaven she will recover her looks in time! Randal will be awfully disgusted if he has to present a tear-stained, pallid, attenuated sufferer to the world as his re-married wife."

"I suppose that would be his feeling," returned Darrell slowly. "I don't quite understand it myself, but I confess I am a little puzzled by Janet—I mean Mrs. Palliser too, she is greatly changed, though physically that will all come right, but there is something absorbing her mind. I trust in God that Palliser has found out her worth during this separation—she is a woman not to be lightly lost."

"Lost! Why, of course he will not lose her! In point of fact, they are as firmly married as ever."

"You think so?" he returned. "It is awfully raw and cold. Let me put this fur rug round you."

CHAPTER IX.

BREAKING AWAY.

THE weather during Lady Saville's visit had
been very variable, one day mild and spring
like, the next chill with a sharp east wind, and
Janet had contrived to take cold. Her father
noticed with some anxiety that her colds
clung to her as they used not to do ; they were
always accompanied by fever, and succeeded
by great weakness. He was much exercised
in his mind by his daughter's mental condition,
she was so patient (patience used not to be a
speciality of hers), so quiet—above all, so
silent.

And now, thought the captain, there was
really nothing to fret about. In a very few
months she would be Mrs. Palliser of Mervyn
again, with all the advantages and privileges

31*

belonging to her station, and probably of
more importance in her husband's eyes
because of the temporary separation. " I
wish the fellow would write a little oftener,
and seemed a little more anxious to come
back to her. No doubt he is, but women are
such fanciful creatures, they want a man to be
saying so all the time—any way, I had better
hold my tongue. I'd only make a mull of it,
for I am a clumsy old chap at best. Why, it's
nearly three weeks since there was a line
from him. I wish she'd write, anyhow. It
does not do to keep a strict debtor account in
such matters, but I'll not meddle."

It was two or three days before Janet left
her room, during which time Mrs. Bent was
constant in her visits. She had had leave of
absence during January to pass a few weeks
with her mother, and she had much to talk
about and describe of the changes and improvements at Langford, which deeply interested Janet.

"I suppose your mother adores your
children?" she observed one afternoon, as

her friend was talking with her over the
bright little fire in her bedroom.

"Yes! they are a great pleasure to the
dear mother, but I really think the Vicar
spoils them more."

"I daresay," returned Janet thoughtfully,
"imagine how my father would have
worshipped a grandson!" She paused and
burst out as if she could not control her
words. "What a terrible misfortune it
would have been if poor little children had
come to us!"

"Don't say that, Janet! They are so sweet,
and—then, who knows? Mr. Palliser is a
man of great influence—something might
have been done to legitimatise them!"

"Nevertheless I am very, *very* glad I
never had any," said Janet with a sigh, and
after a brief pause added, "How much I
should like to see dear Mrs. Winyard once
more."

"She often speaks of you. After all of
us, she loves you best, I am sure! It is
difficult to uproot her, but she has promised

to pay me a visit in May, after Maggie is married."

"And is it fixed?" (the wedding of the Vicar's youngest daughter).

"Yes, for the twentieth of April! I am sure Grace will feel being left the last at home."

"She is a fine, strong, unselfish woman, she will soon get accustomed to it."

"Everyone will be enchanted to get you back, Janet! I fancy you will have even a grander reception than the first."

"Hush!" cried Janet, raising herself in her chair, "I cannot bear to hear of it—I mean, the idea of such excitement makes me ill."

"I am afraid you are very weak, dear," said Mrs. Bent rising, "and I must leave you. This is John's early afternoon, so I like to be at home to give him his tea."

"Yes, of course! I managed to write a letter to Mr. Palliser last night when dear old dad thought I was in bed and asleep— will you post it for me?"

" Certainly ! I hope he was well when you heard from him."

" He seemed in excellent health and spirits."

Mrs. Bent took the letter, kissed her friend and departed.

The next day Janet joined her father at dinner to his great satisfaction. She was looking delicate, but he observed that she was more cheerful and disposed to talk than she had been for some time, and even proposed a hit at backgammon. This improvement encouraged him to break through the rule he had laid down for himself.

" You will write and let Palliser know you are nearly all right again, eh, Jeanie ? " This was an occasional pet name.

" He does not know there was anything the matter with me ! But 1 have written a long letter to him, a letter that has been long on my mind, and it is high time it was written."

" Blowing him up, eh ? " asked the old man, looking keenly at her.

She shook her head with a smile.

" It is too late to talk of it now, but I will
tell you all about it to-morrow. I will come
down directly after breakfast, and——" she
paused.

" You must not tire yourself! "

" No—no—it rests me to talk to you."

*   *   *   *   *

" I have been struggling for courage to
open my heart to you, dear father," began
Janet, when she had descended to the " Den,"
where she found Captain Rowley in a very
restless condition. " So please listen to what
I have to say without exclamations, however
strange it may sound."

" I am sure I am not given to interrupt,"
he ejaculated.

Then there was a silence.

" Is it about your letter ? "

She bent her head.

" You've done something foolish ? "

No answer.

" Come ! what was your letter about ? "

Then the words broke forth :

" My letter ?—my letter was to tell him I will never be his wife again ! "

" His wife !—refused to be his wife ? I don't seem to understand," said the old man with a dazed look.

" Do not be angry with me, dear, dear father ! I am so grieved to vex and disappoint you, but I *cannot* go back to Randal Palliser," said Janet, and her voice showed her mouth was dry with agitation.

" You must have very grave reasons for entertaining so extraordinary an intention ! What are they ? " asked Captain Rowley, with a sudden dignity, as if the depths of his nature had been touched.

Janet could not speak, and he continued, still standing before her :

" I have sometimes feared you were not quite as happy as I could have wished, but —I never would ask a question. Silence is the best mode of healing wounds when a woman is married—but, child ! think of all you forego, think of the injury to yourself, think of the injustice to him—I—I cannot believe you are serious. You've had some tiff with Palliser, and fancy yourself implacable."

"I wish we had had tiffs," exclaimed Janet. "If we had quarrelled and made it up again, we might have loved each other fondly through it all. It was the deadly quiet of Siberian coldness that killed all tenderness, all affection. Ah! believe me, I *have* suffered."

She paused abruptly.

"Have you any reason to think that he was unfaithful to you?" asked Captain Rowley sternly.

"No, such an idea never occurred to me. When we had been a year married I saw a change in him—indeed, I had begun to fear it before, then—then Richard Palliser's son was born, and I had no children. I saw this was an unpardonable failure—I tried, oh! so hard to win him back, to touch him, till I hated myself for my fruitless slavishness. Then I let my own love go, but I hated my position—it humiliated me to be at the head of *his* house, to wear the costly clothes *he*

paid for, to be decked in *his* jewels, all part
of the bargain, in which I had failed to
perform my share! No! no words can
describe the torture of those years, while
Randal grew more and more icy! I know
he looked on me as a useless incumbrance—
so long as I was linked to him irretrievably,
I was determined to keep a fair face to the
world! Had this bondage continued for
some years longer, I should probably have
grown harder and accustomed to it, but now,
when I am still warm, with life vibrating painfully in every nerve, could I resist seizing
this blessed chance?"

Captain Rowley subsided into a large chair,
with a sort of moan.

"But, Janet," he said, "after all, you have
no ill-treatment to complain of; you had
everything you wanted, everything suitable
to your position, and—and you confess you
had no reason to doubt his fidelity."

"I might have *known* he was faithless,
yet forgiven and loved him still, if he had
returned to me with affection and tenderness,

after wandering from the straight road, but without a counter-attraction, he had simply wearied of me, and would willingly have broken away from me if he could. Believe me, I am doing Randal good service."

"My child," he interrupted, "think of the motives that will be attributed to you—everyone will believe you have a lover in the background! And think of the reports that will be spread abroad of Palliser's villainy!"

"The first year will be bad," said Janet steadily, "but we shall both live it down. Before twelve months are over Randal will have found another wife—then, if she gives him a son, he will bless me! Oh, father, dear father," throwing her arms round him, "do not grudge me the first gleam of hope I have had for all these dreary years. Do not turn me from the only real home I have ever known. Let me have the happiness of being with you, of caring for you. No doubt about my rights in *your* house. Let me have peace, my dear father!" and she burst into a passionate fit of weeping.

The old man was quite overcome. He held her to his heart, and uttered confused sentences.

"It's an awful business. I never heard of anything like it. Send you away, my precious pet?—not likely, when you are the light of my eyes! You know you are just setting law and religion at defiance. You, a well-brought-up girl. I am sure I hadn't a notion that Palliser was a cold-blooded rascal of that sort. My God! that he should have made you miserable! Don't cry, dear, you shall do just as you like, only I will not hear of your deciding all of a sudden; take time, my pet."

"I have taken time, dearest Dad. I have been studying this step for months, and, as it affects Randal too. I will never return to the man who was my husband. I shall make my existence somehow, even if *you* turn me out. If you let me stay, I will not cost you much."

"Cost *me* much. My child, you are worth your weight in gold to me, and I am better off than I used to be. These years, while I had only my own old self to pay for, I saved up a bit, and invested a trifle; Tom managed that for me. Oh, Lord, what *will* Mrs. Tom say?"

"It does not matter much, dear; we'll go away somewhere together, and after a while I shall forget I was ever married—ever anything but Janet Rowley."

"Ah, but you'll not forget so easily. Child, you have not counted the cost of such an— an outrageous act. Why—why did you not consult me before you committed yourself in writing?"

"Because, dear, I knew you would oppose me, so I wished to commit myself first. Father, I thought out this resolution with all the force of my heart and brain, and I shall not be diverted from it. My deepest regret is to cause you pain, but when that is past, you too will be far, far happier—so will Randal. Dearest father, I cannot go back to my former life."

The old man walked distractedly to and fro.

"How will you stand the—the sort of disgrace, Janet?" he cried. "To have lived nearly five years with a man, and then to proclaim to the world that you don't mind the disgrace of being no wife at all."

"I neither see nor feel the disgrace of it. You will have no cause to be ashamed of me."

There was a few moments' silence, then Captain Rowley came to the fire-place and stood still.

"Look here, Janet," he said more composedly, "I am not going to speak another word on the subject until we see what Palliser has to say for himself. No, not another word. You must have more to complain of than you admit, but whatever happens, try to be just to your husband. Yes, he *is* your husband. If his own conscience does not condemn him, he'll find it deuced hard to forgive such a proposition as you have made, but, we'll see, so say no more at present."

"Very well; it is perhaps wiser. I will

leave you now, dear, for I feel tired and shaken, and——"

Her voice failed.

"Child," he exclaimed, "don't wear yourself out with unnecessary troubles, and, my darling, you may believe that, right or wrong, your old Dad will stick to you through thick and thin."

She threw her arms round him, and kissed his rather rugged face lovingly, then went quickly to her room to compose herself before they met again.

Thank God, the ice was broken—now there could be no drawing back. A little more courage and endurance, and the links which bound her to the past would be broken, and she might begin a new life—a very quiet and obscure one, but peaceful, and unembittered by the sense of being in a false position, of being an unprofitable partner, who had failed to fulfil her share of the agreement, which had been a canker to her soul.

"Will Gertrude or Lady Darrell have anything to do with me when they know?" she thought. "Shall I have strength to stand alone? I firmly believe I am doing right. If there was the faintest hope of being of any real use to Randal, I should not hesitate, but he will be better in every way without me. He will feel that at once, but he will be terribly vexed all the same, and when the fight is over——What a long stretch of life lies before me! It is not exhilarating to think of, but I do not fear. I shall find my niche, I shall find work. How I wish the next month were over!"

*   *   *   *   *

Captain Rowley was not a man of exalted intellect, nor of angelic character, but he had a stout backbone and a clear idea of right and wrong. He kept strictly to his determination, not to speak on the subject of his daughter's extraordinary resolution to break with Palliser. But it was never absent from the mind of either of them. This naturally put a drag on their conversation, so time went all the slower, as each privately counted the days which must intervene before Janet could have a reply.

She kept much indoors, and rather avoided her friend, Mrs. Bent, feeling that, for the present, she was a species of impostor. As the days dropped one by one into the abyss of the past like leaden weights, both father and daughter grew more restless and more silent, occasionally an expressive hand pressure passed between them, and there was something of solemn tenderness in the tone with which he added, " And God bless you," to his usual " Good-night."

A week or more had passed since Janet's fatal letter was sent, when, in the late afternoon a telegram was brought to her :

" Alexandria,
Feb. —'89.

" Yours just received. I start by the English mail steamer for Brindisi to-morrow morning, to reply in person."

The paper fell from her hand. The battle

was then imminent; she must be true to herself. If she could only escape giving Randal pain! The bitterness she used at times to feel seemed to have passed out of her heart; she only wanted to be free, not to hurt anyone.

"It will soon be over," she told herself encouragingly, and then?—would it be the peace of death?

When Captain Rowley (who had been out for his usual "constitutional") returned, Janet gave him the telegram without a word. He read it carefully, and then, to Janet's surprise, said in a tone of some exultation:

"By George, you *have* stirred him up. Now, my pet, promise me to hear all he has to say steadily and impartially."

"Yes!" returned Janet very deliberately, "I can promise so much."

The days which succeeded seemed longer than ever, Janet could scarcely eat or sleep, and Captain Rowley was not much better. Finally, before she thought he could have reached England, as she sat trying to do some needlework (for reading was quite out

32*

of the question), the drawing-room door was opened and Mrs. Brown—"General Brown," as Captain Rowley called her, because she was a general servant, announced in a joyous tone :

"Mr. Palliser, ma'am !"

He entered quickly, looking embrowned and remarkably well, alert, distinguished, with an irresistible air.

"Janet !" he exclaimed, and paused in his approach. "Why, Janet, have you been ill? You ought to have told me."

He looked keenly at her, but did not offer his hand.

"Not seriously ill," she returned rising, though feeling for a moment blind, and deaf, and dizzy, with a terrible sensation of faintness. "I have only had a succession of colds, and you, Randal — you seem remarkably well?"

"Yes, I am all right, only somewhat done up after a very hurried journey. I have come to answer your insane letter in person ! Pray was it written in the delirium of fever?"

he went on in a contemptuous tone, "or—
what does it mean?" and he drew a chair,
facing her with great composure.

"What it expresses, Randal. I do not wish
to be your wife again."

"I am afraid the long nervous strain has
been too much for you? Has it induced
softening of the brain?" he said coldly.

"Rather hardening of the heart, in the
sense of strengthening it," returned Janet
steadily, for having made the beginning,
she felt her courage rise. "Do not think I
am speaking from any weak or passionate
impulse. I have thought of this for months!"

"Who is my rival?" exclaimed Palliser
fiercely. "What fresh humiliation have you
planned for me? Is this your return for the
tenderness, the luxury, I have heaped upon
you?"

"You have no rival, Randal! God knows
I do not want to injure you! I shall injure
myself much more — but you have long
ceased to love me, and I have failed to fulfil
your dearest wish. I am 'an unprofitable

servant,' my own affection is frozen out—why
—for want of a little courage, should we
either of us go back into bondage? Why try
to mend up our 'broken links'?"

She was quite herself now, and conveyed
a sudden impression of resolute purpose,
which astonished Palliser.

"You are mad, decidedly mad," he
exclaimed, pacing the room after the fashion
of perplexed men. "If you persist in this
unpardonable folly, people will say that I
have treated you brutally, in spite of my
seeming a gentleman! I shall not be left a
shred of character!"

"I shall always speak well of you, Randal!
You were never brutal! You could not be!
You only pierced, you did not crush! You
ceased to love me—why—you could not tell
probably. My love died harder because of
its own nature, I suppose—and therefore I
suffered more pain. So much pain—that if
—if you could have understood, you might
have been more merciful! You see no
grandeur, nor success, nor wealth, could

make up for the want of which—of what you perhaps could not give; but that is all over now, my love is quite dead too. I will never be your wife again."

"By Heaven, Janet! I cannot fathom your motives—you have some secret motive, I am convinced?"

"Yes!—a strong one. I want to secure peace and self-respect. In your house I could have neither."

"But, Janet! Try to be reasonable, try to be like other people. In sober seriousness, what have you to complain of? Have I ever denied you anything you ever wished for? Have I not rather anticipated your wishes? Have you not had the fullest advantage of your position as my wife? You ought to know by this time, that the effervescence of passion *cannot* last! I did my best to bear what was a cruel disappointment, and though you must have known what a constant source of bitterness it was to me——"

"And to me," interrupted Janet in a low tone. "Do you think I was ever for a moment unconscious of your disappointment? Do you think you possess any mental plummet by which you could sound the depth, the intensity of my cruel mortification, my sense of absolute guilt towards you? This surely can account for my eagerness to set you free? Believe me, I am as anxious to give *you* freedom as to secure it for myself!"

"And what is to become of you, if you carry out this amazing scheme? Will you settle down into poverty and obscurity?"

"Yes! I shall return to the place from whence I came."

"But don't you, as a religious woman, feel yourself bound by those solemn words, 'Whom God hath joined together let not man put asunder'?"

"Which of your wives did God especially join you to, Randal?" she asked, a sad smile passing over her lips. "Would the sanctity of our vows have saved me harmless, had I remained with you when that wretched woman reappeared? Accident has played sad havoc with the holiness of the tie which bound us."

" Your selfishness will ruin me !" exclaimed Palliser, pausing in his troubled walk. " Men will shun me—aye, and women too, when they reckon *all* you renounce, rather than return to me !"

"No, Randal, no ! Before a year is over you will be accepted as kindly as ever in Society, and fair women will be as ready to marry you, for you have everything— reputation, wealth, station, charm—ah ! how much charm I once knew well !"

She raised her eyes to his with something of the old tenderness in their gaze.

A curious thrill ran through his veins.

" Janet ! you have been foolishly exacting ! A man cannot always be a lover, even to so sweet a woman as you are. Can you believe I am indifferent to you, dearest ?" drawing a chair beside her and taking her hand— " If you look into my eyes——"

Janet smiling, interrupted him.

" No, I do not believe it, Randal, I *know* it.

I do not blame you, I suppose it is involuntary, only—of all the manifestations I have experienced from you, none have ever estranged me so much as your passing fits of caressing fondness which to - morrow turned to dust and ashes; I have no enmity to you, Randal—how could you give me what you do not possess? But it would be madness not to grasp this chance of freedom!"

"I will plead no more," cried Palliser, rising, white with rage and mortification, his momentary feeling of tenderness vanishing. "I suppose you have taken into consideration the effect this disastrous decision will have upon your father?"

"I have," she returned sadly. "It will distress him, I fear, but on my head be it."

"Very well," said Palliser sternly, "I give you a week to reconsider the matter; at the end of that time, should you continue in the same mind—we part—for ever."

"In a week," said Janet, steadily, "I will in any case write to you."

Palliser stood silent for a moment and then said :

"I must see Captain Rowley ; he cannot approve of this mad determination ! He will tell you what a deathblow this will be to your own reputation."

"I think my reputation will survive ; but I will send my father to you ! So it is good-bye, Randal ? "

" Not till you have written finally ! "

Janet bent her head and left the room.

Having summoned Captain Rowley who obeyed with alacrity, she went quickly on to the privacy of her own chamber. She was profoundly moved. The past, with all the sweetness and enchantment of first love, of unstinted faith in " the long, sunny lapse of a summer's daylight," glowing with tenderness and affection, came back to her, melting her heart with its memory of intoxicating happiness.

What would she not have given to be able to trust Randal and believe in him as she once did !

But the worst was now over, she was nervously anxious for her father's report of his interview with Palliser — it would be painful, of course! How she wished the good old man could be spared this sore trial?—but once over, he should have the comfort of her care, her company, for the rest of his days, and after——— The question rose swiftly as a flash of vivid lightning, that suddenly reveals a bleak and dreary moor—would hers be a desolate, lonely life?

The sound of a door closing with some violence, startled her, and the next moment a tap on her own door announced Captain Rowley.

His face was flushed, his air disturbed. He did not speak for a moment, but came across the room and stood by the fire, looking away to the window, evidently seeing nothing.

"He's gone!" said he at length; "it's a bad business, Janet! I did not think you would have been so obstinate. Palliser is deeply offended, and we cannot wonder—I don't suppose a greater affront was ever put on a man. In short, he lost all self-control, and said many things that had been better left unsaid. I do not know that I should recommend you to return to him *now*, unless indeed you come round at once before any whisper of your intention gets out. My child! you must have some stronger reason for such a desperate step than any you have told me. I am not asking your reasons, I have faith in you, and I do not believe you would make such a proposition without sufficient cause. So, my dear, though I would advise you to reconsider the matter carefully before you give Palliser the final answer he demands, I shall interfere no further. You are the best of daughters, and I shall stand by you, come what may."

"Then I fear nothing!" cried Janet, clasping her arms round him; "this is a rough passage, dearest, but we'll get into smooth waters by-and-bye, and spend many a peaceful day together."

*　　　*　　　*　　　*　　　*

Punctually at the date appointed, Palliser received the following :

"I write as I promised. I am still in the same mind, Randal ; we shall probably never meet again, at least I hope not, for I could never see you without emotion. I do not blame you for ceasing to love me, I suppose you could not help it. I only pity myself, because I have lost both your love and my own. I hope and believe that you will yet thank me for the step I am taking. Though I leave you, I am still

"Yours faithfully,
"JANET ROWLEY."

END OF VOL. II.